LISTEN
FOR THE FIG TREE

Behold the fig tree,
and all the trees; when they shoot forth,
Ye see and know of your own selves
that summer is nigh at hand.

—JESUS OF NAZARETH

LISTEN
FOR THE FIG TREE

SHARON BELL MATHIS

THE VIKING PRESS NEW YORK

In Appreciation

I wish to thank G. J. DeAngelis, Director of Services, Columbia Lighthouse for the Blind, Washington, D.C., for his kindness and his willingness to give me the information that I needed to write this book.

Acknowledgments:

Page 6: Reprinted by permission of Julian Bach Literary Agency, Inc. Copyright © 1974 by June Jordan.
Page 156: *Black Song: The Forge and The Flame*, John Lovell, Jr., The Macmillan Company, New York, N.Y., 1972.

First published in 1974 by The Viking Press, Inc.
625 Madison Avenue, New York, N.Y. 10022
Published simultaneously in Canada by
The Macmillan Company of Canada Limited
Printed in U.S.A.

2 3 4 5 78 77 76 75

Library of Congress Cataloging in Publication Data

Mathis, Sharon Bell. Listen for the fig tree.

summary: A sixteen-year-old black girl's first celebration of Kwanza gives her a sense of the past and strength to deal with her troubled mother and her own blindness. [1. Blind—Fiction. 2. Family problems—Fiction. 3. Negroes—Social conditions—Fiction] I. Title. PZ7.M4284Li [Fic] 73–19797
ISBN 0–670–43016–1

This book is dedicated to nine Beautiful, Tell-It-Like-It-Is, Black women: my mother, ALICE FRAZIER BELL, who made a way out of no way for us; my sisters, PAT and MARCIA; BEATRICE KIDD JACKSON and her daughter CAROLYN; EMMA A. EDWARDS; LUCY THOMAS; MARY HARRIS; and for my beloved godmother, BERTHA REED McDONALD, who collected the stories and poems I wrote as a little girl and who said to me, "*Put my name in one of your books and let me see it before I die.*"

"So Brooklyn has become a holy place..."

JUNE JORDAN
On the Death of Michael Angelo Thompson

ONE

"WILL YOU PLEASE don't go out, Momma," Muffin pleaded, still blocking the door.

Whisky. Sweet, sour smell. Pushing down the air about her mother. Stuffy, stink-of-whisky smell.

Better not to see, Muffin thought. Better to reach out and touch and feel when you wanted to.

"Move, Marvina!"

"But it's real late, Momma, and a few minutes ago you said you were going to bed." Muffin moved closer to the smell of her mother and touched her bony shoulder for only a moment before the woman pulled away sharply, missed her footing, and fell backward. "Please, Momma," Muffin managed to say, moving forward, reaching for her mother and hearing the crack of her back against the slick, highly enameled hallway wall. "Please, Momma," Muffin begged. "You hurt yourself— you okay? Please stay home."

"Shut up, Marvina! I ain't hurt, I'm going!"

Muffin reached out and touched the huge, worn, ribbed cotton collar zipped up and still gaping open about her mother's small neck. "And you don't even have your good coat on, Momma, and it's cold out and all you have on is Daddy's thin old jacket. I can feel it, Momma! It's too cold for you to go out like that!"

Muffin felt her mother flip up her arms and push her fingers away. "Don't be feeling on me—if I got on this jacket, don't you worry. You can't see—how you going to tell if I'm warm, Marvina! This your father's jacket, this Marvin's jacket! If it's all right on him, then it's all right on me! Now! How you like that?"

"Momma, please go to bed."

"What I need to go to bed for?" Leola Johnson yelled, trying to step around her daughter. "You go to bed! Go to bed your ownself. Now move! Move out my way, Marvina!"

Where was Mr. Dale? Muffin thought, worrying again. It was time for him to come down the steps on his way to the Midnight Club. But she remembered she hadn't talked to him all day, hadn't heard him at all, though she had listened hard for the muffled, quick clump clump of his high-heeled boots on the hallway carpet.

"Marvina, move!"

But Muffin didn't move in the darkness about her. She was listening to the signs in her mother's voice and the signs in her mother's movements which told her how difficult the night would be. In this almost year since her father's murder, she had learned to depend on what she sensed in the too-excited voice or the too-quiet crying, the no-talking-at-all days, and now the frequent all around smell of whisky.

"Now you just going to stand there when you hear

me saying move to you? You hear me—you hear me telling you move?"

"It's after twelve-thirty at night, Momma," Muffin said, opening the glass bubble dome and touching the dial of the Braille watch she wore. "It's too late for you to go out. I'm scared if you go out."

"Keep on being scared. I'm going," Leola mumbled, trying to pull Muffin's hand away from the doorknob. Then she pushed hard at Muffin's fingers, but the girl held tight, didn't let go. "Get from the damn doorway, Marvina, damn it!"

"Please go to bed, Momma."

"No!"

"Why?"

"Why! What I got to go to bed for! I ain't got nobody to sleep with—tell me I got somebody to sleep with—tell me your father still alive. Tell me that!" Leola snapped her fingers close to Muffin's ears, and the sharp sound of the bony fingers took its place in a corner of Muffin's mind with the other brittle, quick-changing sounds of her mother. "Tell me the cops didn't let him bleed to death like a damn dog!" Snapping fingers, louder this time, more brittle, closer. "Just like that! That's how they let him die! On Christmas Day—or Kwanza—whatever you always talking about! Talk, talk, talk! If you got to talk, talk about how your father was murdered twice! Murdered *two* damn times!"

"You didn't take your medicine today, Momma."

"You take it."

"That's why you're so excited, Momma. You didn't take your medicine."

9

"I'm excited because you got your long legs stretched cross the doorway. You can't see nothing—but you know how to stretch your legs cross things to block my way! Plus, I ain't excited, I'm drunk!"

"You're not drunk, Momma."

"I'll be drunk when I come back, drunk as I want! And I know you don't like it and you got to go in your embarrassment bag—but you being embarrassed don't mean that much to me—" Snapped fingers again. Not quick. But a slow-down deliberate pop Muffin felt close to her lips. "Don't mean *nothing*! Ain't no sign of nothing! Get embarrassed some more. Cause I'm getting drunk some more!"

Where was Mr. Dale?

"Plus I'm going to ask you one more time, Marvina—did my check come?"

"No," Muffin said carefully.

"You lying, I know you lying! And I'm going over to Willie's Jesus church and ask him and he better not tell me you took my check around there today. Cause I know it came. Look simple as you want but I know it came, and if he tells me you took it around there and cashed it—you in trouble. You in trouble, you hear me!"

Muffin wasn't sure why she stepped away from the door then, but she did. Moved away from the smell of varnished doorframe, stepped off the braided rag-strip doormat she had made when she was ten, when glaucoma finally closed out light from the darkening screens that were her eyes. Making treasures of the colors and places and faces she remembered—and locking out the new.

10   Leola tried to slam the door, but Muffin wouldn't

let her and closed it herself and leaned against it and felt the hardness growing in her throat and the cold draft from the door against her face. She listened to her mother go down the steps fussing.

"Got her legs all stretched like she got no sense. Blocking my way! She not the mother, *I'm* the mother!"

After a while the scratched splinter-edged door felt colder pressed against Muffin's face and she left it, still wet with her tears, and walked back to the kitchen and knew the overhead light was on and turned it off and went into her bedroom and closed the door behind and didn't turn the dresser lamp on and was glad for the darkness. She sat down on the bed.

Moments later, Muffin flipped open the watch dome and didn't feel the dial and closed it and opened it again. Her father had given her the Braille watch when she was six, though she had been able to see some. A few months ago, on her sixteenth birthday, Mr. Dale had given her a new wide suede watchband. Lately, Muffin found herself rubbing the velvety leather. Letting her fingers smooth the fine sleek texture. But then suddenly dragging her fingers backward against the grain, feeling the bits of leather recoil.

Muffin felt the dial and closed it. One A.M. Tuesday. Exactly five more days before Saturday. Christmas. The day, last year, when her father was killed.

And six days before Kwanza. Beginning one moment after midnight on Christmas Day.

But it was too hard to think about the African celebration while her mother was out in the street. Too hard now to remember the many months she had helped

11

with the planning for it at the Black Museum. And the hundreds of shapes she had cut out of black paper and sprinkled with runny, too-long-drying glue and tiny, gritty, finger-clinging sparkles. It didn't matter that she wouldn't see the mobiles hanging from the ceiling. She'd know they were up there.

Just as she knew these terrible weeks for her mother would end as soon as Christmas was over.

Her mother would stop drinking then, stop putting the half-pint bottles in the headboard or under the bed or just behind the spread that hung folded from the pillow. When Christmas was over, things would be all right again. Maybe her mother would even go back to the clinic, listen to the doctors, take her medicine the way she was supposed to. Miss Geneva had told her not to worry. "Your mother's having it read bad," she had said a few days ago, "getting through this Christmas. You just have to pay her no mind like I do when she comes to me and tells me she sees him again and carrying on the way she do. I just say to her, 'Leola, don't talk foolish. People think you losing your mind and you got that child and you worrying her half to death.' But that's just what I say to her but I'm telling you she be all right. Don't you worry," Miss Geneva had told her. "If she act up too much, come downstairs and get me."

But going down to get Miss Geneva didn't help, and most of the time her mother would say things to make Miss Geneva cry.

"*How you going to tell me how to feel about my husband, Geneva! You never had no kind of husband.*"

12 *You get yourself a husband first and then you and me*

can talk. Only thing you know is taking care other people's children and you never had none of your own and you can't tell me what to do with the one I got. Me and Marvin. You supposed to be alone. I ain't supposed to be alone. I'm supposed to have a husband. You want to say something, say something to bring my husband back and don't be worrying about my drinking!"

"What about the child?"

"Marvina all right. Don't you worry about Marvina."

"She's blind, Leola. She need you to see what's going on."

"Marvina doing okay. Marvina doing better than you. Marvina got a boy come here every day to see if she okay and keeps a funny-looking, broken-down car to take her to school every morning. Don't you worry about Marvina. Marvina doing a hell of a lot better than you!"

When Muffin read two o'clock on her watch she got up from the bed and opened her closet and reached for her navy blue pea jacket and lay it on the foot of the bed and opened her top dresser drawer and took out the navy blue hat she had crocheted in a shell design for her mother's birthday. Her mother hadn't worn it, saving it with everything else, and Muffin had worn it once and then more and more until finally it wasn't necessary to put it back in her mother's dresser any more.

Muffin went back to the closet again and counted over six dresses and found the green corduroy jumper and pulled it quickly over her nightgown and reached on the left side of the top ledge where her father had built special compartments for her and took down the first sweater she felt, the old green one with the turtleneck stretched too wide. It would do. She pulled it on and reached for her coat and put that on too and stuck her feet in her loafers. Then Muffin stood in front of the mirror and put on the crocheted hat and felt to make sure she didn't have any hair sticking through the design. Her Afro had grown too long and she had meant to have it reshaped, but too much had happened in the last few weeks and her hair hadn't been important. It was never important to her. Only to Mr. Dale. And since she would see him shortly she reached up and patted her hat and her hair once more before she put on her dark glasses and unhooked the wooden cane, covered with deeply cut-in names and initials, from the base of the wooden pineapple tip of the bedpost on the right side of her headboard.

Ernie had dug out the letters with the point of his penknife last summer at Coney Island. She had lain there on his father's old army blanket and felt the sun drying the expensive denim bathing suit Mr. Dale had bought for her and which caused her skin to itch, and felt good that Ernie was enjoying cutting in the initials. "Deeta's are skinny to go with her legs," he had said. And later, that same evening, he had repainted the cane with fast-drying white enamel and red for the bottom. "And I put a small green band and a small black band where the red first begins," he had said, "so the people know you got your head together."

Muffin took her eyeglasses off the plastic tusks of a small felt baby elephant that Miss Geneva had brought back from North Carolina for her.

And for a moment Muffin allowed herself to think

about the dog she would be able to have as soon as she turned eighteen. "Black Cinque," Mr. Dale always called him. "Prince of Amistad. The biggest, blackest shepherd money can buy—and I'm buying and I'm buying the best! The other Seeing Eye dogs gonna bow when he comes by, gonna salute!" It didn't seem to matter to Mr. Dale that she'd probably have to have a spayed female, he just kept saying "Black Cinque. Prince of Amistad!"

Well, Black Cinque, Prince of Amistad, Muffin said to herself after she had bolted her door and was walking down the steps, at least by the time you get here Momma won't be doing all this. In a way, I wish Christmases never came again.

Muffin could hear Mr. Dale's stereo playing upstairs though she knew he wasn't home. He kept it on, he told her, so people wouldn't know whether he was home or not.

Except for the music and Muffin's cane touching the carpeted steps, the hall was soundless. It was even too late for Mr. Thomas to open his door and peep out. He was probably asleep in his apartment, Muffin thought, probably sleeping in a real old bed that smelled old, too. Like his apartment smelled whenever he opened the door, even if he only opened it a little way.

Tank wasn't in the hall either.

Muffin opened the door leading to the street then and walked out. The quiet outside felt larger.

Icy Brooklyn wind cut into her face and her neck and her ankles.

Momma's cold, she thought and walked like she always did, close to the buildings. Except when she came to Deeta's house she didn't reach up the way she usually did and rub her hand over the cracked mane of the only stone lion left on the block. Muffin turned the corner.

"Hi, Miss Cupcakes, Miss Pie! Hi!"

It was Tank.

"Tank so messed up with them drugs and stuff," Miss Geneva had said, "he don't know what the year is, let alone the time. All he do is walk and sit and act crazy, dying on his feet. In and out halls all day long."

"Hi, Tank," Muffin answered and wondered why he wasn't standing inside somewhere instead of standing out in the cold. Maybe he really was mixed up about things.

"You all right?"

"I'm okay, Tank," Muffin called back and kept walking, her cane barely touching the bumps and cracks she knew so well in the cement sidewalk on this side of Reid Avenue. The large split in the pavement now. Only a few more steps to the New Church, which she knew was closed. But that didn't matter. The person in charge wasn't.

Mr. Willie Williams. Her father's best friend.

Muffin tried the church door anyway before she rang the bell to Mr. Willie Williams' apartment above the storefront church. Then she moved back a little and looked up so that when Mr. Willie Williams came to the window and called down like he usually did, he would see her quickly.

Her ankles were freezing and Muffin was glad when she finally heard Mr. Willie Williams come bounding down the narrow hallway steps and open the door. "Muff," he said. "What's the matter? Where's Leola?"

"I don't know," Muffin said. "She went out a little while ago, and I didn't know if she was coming here or if she was going to Mr. Dale's. The only thing is I haven't seen him all day and maybe he didn't even go to his club. So I came here first, and maybe we can go to Mr. Dale's and if she's not there maybe we can go to the cab company. She might be sitting over there again." Muffin thought the cold was passing through her bones and she hunched her shoulders up a little, though that didn't help. "And I know Momma's freezing because she's only got on that thin jacket Daddy used to wear all the time and she was drinking and she might go some place where nobody knows her. You know Momma says a lot of things and maybe somebody won't like what she says to them and—"

"And I told you not to come out no more looking for Leola. You shouldn't had that telephone cut off, you need a telephone, Muff. You just can't keep coming out late like this. You just can't do it."

"But you know what Momma was doing—Momma was calling people down in Nashville and talking about Daddy and stuff like that all the time, and I couldn't get her off the phone. And if people hung up—she'd call them right back. The telephone cost too much."

"Damn shame. She's got you walking around half the night like this."

Mr. Willie Williams was the only preacher Muffin knew who cursed.

"This ain't the country," he was saying while they

17

were in his apartment and she heard him putting on his coat. "People up here don't know you—you can't just walk around here when it's night. Your father and me grew up together and he wouldn't like this none at all. Not for one damn minute would he like it. Leola's gone stone crazy. She never knew what liquor was till a month ago!"

When they arrived at the Midnight Club, Mr. Willie Williams opened the door, and then he closed it. "She's in there," he said.

"I'm glad," Muffin said and knew Mr. Willie Williams wouldn't go in and her mother wasn't about to come out. "At least we don't have to go over to the cab company where Daddy used to work. It was real hard last time when we tried to get her out of there." Muffin pulled open the nail-studded metal door. "I don't think Momma's going to come out, Mr. Willie Williams," she said. "So I'm going to stay here with her and when Mr. Dale comes to lock up, he'll walk us home. If he doesn't come back, it's okay. I'm not scared. You don't have to wait for us. Momma'll be all right."

"Muff, he can't close till four, and he don't have to come back." Muffin heard Mr. Willie Williams curse under his breath. "I could march in there and bring her out," he said almost to himself. "She don't weigh much as a bird. But she got so much mouth!" He put his arm about Muffin's shoulders and she felt him shake his head. "I just don't want you being hurt by her cursing and carrying on. I swear fore God I'll be glad when this thing passes for her, this Christmas comes and goes, so she don't go way down."

"Shut the damn door," a woman yelled from inside. "I ain't no polar bear!"

"You go on in with her," Mr. Willie Williams said. "I'll stay out here."

"Hey, Leola! It's your kid. Ain't that your kid?"

"Tell the *kid* to shut the damn door," the woman yelled again. Muffin heard her mother curse the woman, heard her rushing forward to where she stood, and Muffin turned, her cane tip probing quickly in front of her, and walked back outside to Mr. Willie Williams' side. Once her mother was outside, it might be possible to get her to go home.

"Marvina!"

Before Muffin could answer, her mother came out. "Don't come around me with no Jesus talk," Muffin heard her yell very close to Mr. Willie Williams and close to her. "Somebody come with that talk tonight, they in trouble!"

"I'm not talking to you, Leola. I got nothing to say to you tonight. I'm just here to see Muff get back home all right. And see you get back all right."

"Drop dead," Leola shrieked. "You don't have to see me and Marvina do nothing. Go preach!" she yelled. "Go preach, go preach!"

Muffin felt her mother's hands on her face, rubbing her cheeks. "You cold, baby?" she asked, leaning a little on Muffin. The old jacket she wore felt thin next to the girl's heavy one. "Baby—you cold?"

"No, Momma," Muffin said.

But Leola pulled Muffin's coat collar closer up around her neck anyway and looked for more buttons to button and couldn't find any and stood there holding her daughter tightly around the waist, her face on Muffin's neck.

"You near ready to go home, Leola?"

"No!"

"Muff's got to get up and go to school—go home with her and the two of you, you and her, go home and go to sleep."

"She ain't worrying about no school. She's smart—only thing is she can't see. Marvina's blind. You know Marvina blind!" Muffin, standing close to Mr. Willie Williams, felt her mother's warm, sour breath in her face. "She been going blind since she was born but she ain't got no nasty-looking eyes—I'll tell you that! Yeah, Marvina can't see but she don't have to wear them glasses can't nobody see through. Marvina just do that cause she want. Marvina's eyes look gooder than yours!"

"Momma," Muffin said, pulling away carefully from her mother. "Are we walking home with Mr. Willie Williams or are we waiting for Mr. Dale? If we're going home with Mr. Dale—if you're not ready to go—let's go inside and let Mr. Willie Williams go home and get some sleep."

"Willie don't sleep. All Willie do is pray," Leola said and kissed Muffin on the lips. "My sweet baby," she said. "Just like her father. My Marvin. Wasn't he my Marvin, Willie? He was my Marvin. I never had no other boyfriend or nothing. It was just Marvin and me all my life and now he's gone and I ain't got nothing."

"How can you stand up here and say you got nothing

and hugging onto that child like that? You got Muff—Muff's your daughter, you got a child!"

"She just says that, Mr. Willie Williams," Muffin said.

The nail-studded door opened and closed and people were coming out to look at them and Muffin clutched her cane and wanted to knock them away with it, to push them out of her life and away from her mother. She could see their faces in her darkness. A man drunk and talking. "Leola's girl blind, can't see a lick. Hard luck."

Another man answering, "You hard luck too."

"I'm tired of people saying what I got," Leola screamed. "The damn doctors at the clinic get on my nerves with that damn business! You got a daughter they say—stop saying you ain't got nothing!" She changed her voice to mimic the doctors and then switched back to her own voice. "They got to jump back," she said. "They don't mess with me at that clinic. All I say is, who gave me my daughter? That's what I say, who gave me my daughter! *Maaarrvin* did! I want both, I say. Give me both or shut up. Yeah, I got Marvina, I know I got Marvina. I want Marvin too. Marvin and Marvina." Leola kissed Muffin then and hugged her hard.

"Damn," Muffin heard somebody say and then go back inside the club. "Damn!"

Leola reached up and kissed Muffin again and the cane tip pressed on Muffin's ankle and cut in. She shifted it from between her and her mother. Her mother didn't seem to notice. "Marvina! Your cheeks so cold. What you doing so cold?"

21

"You feel cold too, Momma," Muffin managed to say.

"I ain't cold. I ain't never been no cold woman."

"Leola!"

"Willie, who you hollering at!"

"Momma," Muffin said quickly. "Let's go back inside if you want to and Mr. Willie Williams can go back home. We just wanted to see if you were all right."

"No! Hell, no! He didn't come to see if I was okay, Willie came to preach! Go ahead, Willie," Muffin heard her mother scream. "Preach, Jesus. Tell Jesus I want my husband back. Tell Him I can't do nothing right no more and while you at it—tell Him I'm coming on soon and when I get there Marvin better be okay. His head better not be this big no more, all bashed in and swelling. You hear me, Preacher Willie? Tell Jesus what I say!" Then Muffin heard her mother punch Mr. Willie Williams' arm. "Plus, nobody's going home or nowhere else till you and Marvina prove you ain't got my check!"

"We can talk tomorrow, Leola," Mr. Willie Williams said.

"Talk, hell! You and Marvina got my money!"

Mr. Willie Williams was trying to calm her mother down when a car pulled up and stopped and Muffin heard what she had been listening for all evening, all night.

"Sweet Black Muffin child. Plum of my life. Let's go home."

It was Mr. Dale.

TWO

"BE A YEAR SOON, DALE," Muffin heard her
mother say softly, twenty minutes later when they were
back in the apartment. "This Saturday coming, Christmas, be a year."

Mr. Dale, his arm about Muffin's waist, was whispering to her. "Go to bed, sweet angel," he said.

But when Muffin walked away Mr. Dale called her
back sharply. "My God!" he shrieked. "You're slouch-
ing! For God's sake, Muffin, don't slouch! Strut with
that cane, strut!"

"Marvina don't need nobody's cane when I'm round,
she don't need no damn cane in here! Marvina know
where everything at in this house. Marvin too! The only
one don't know from nothing is me. Marvina, give me
that damn cane! Marvina, you hear me! Dale!" Muffin
heard her mother smack Mr. Dale. "Dale! Get me that
damn scratched-up piece of wood—Marvina got that
name mess all over it! Marvina, come back in here!
Marvina! Marvina! See that, Dale. There she go. There
she go—tap, tap, tap! Marvina doing all that tapping but
Marvina got my money!"

"Leola, will you shut up! What would that sweet angel want with your money—you ain't *got* no money worth taking!"

"Soon's I get myself together and that ain't going to be never either—I'm getting on Preaching Willie's case!" Muffin heard her mother yell. "Willie got Marvina doing all this mess!"

Then Muffin heard her mother call down the hall, "Slouch much as you want, baby—much as you want to. Dale wish he knew how to slouch like you slouch!" Leola snapped her finger loud. "Do it, Marvina," she said and Muffin heard her smack Mr. Dale again. "You wish you could slouch good as Marvina slouch!"

Muffin lay in bed listening to her mother fussing with Mr. Dale. "How you going to tell me what to stop doing, Dale? How you trying to do that! Get out my house. Get off sitting on my bed! That's Marvin's side—don't you light on it! You know that's Marvin's side. You know you know it!"

A short time later, when Mr. Dale had gone, Muffin was awakened by her mother. She felt the thin jacket hang down in her face, her mother was still wearing it. "Marvina, wake up! I can't sleep. Marvina, wake up—where's my medicine? Where you put it, Marvina!"

Muffin didn't move.

"Marvina!"

"You can't have your medicine, Momma."

"Marvina, damn it—don't start that mess. I ain't never took away nothing you need. I ever take your cane and throw it out the window? Marvina! I ever tell you not to use that damn cane just cause I can't stand that tapping? Marvina, wait, baby—get up and talk to me. Momma don't mean to yell—you know I don't mean to fuss or nothing, Marvina. Marvina, you listening to Momma?"

"I'm listening, Momma, but you can't have the pills. You know you can't have them when you've been drinking that whisky."

"I got to sleep, baby."

Muffin didn't answer. She felt her mother's warm kisses on her face and in her hair. She felt her mother's tears running down her neck, and still she didn't move.

"If I'm not drinking or taking some pills or sleeping, I keep seeing your father. You lucky, Marvina. You lucky you couldn't see it. I ain't never going to forget how he looked and he knew we were there—you and me. I could tell by his eyes he knew. And he knew they were just letting him lay there and die. It was the cops let him die while they asked questions and never called no ambulance—cause he was Black! They let him lay there and die like that. If he was white, they wouldn't have let the ground touch him two seconds before they would of had him up! But he was Black, Marvina. Marvina!"

"Yes, Momma."

"You sleep?"

"No, Momma."

"You won't get my medicine so I got to talk."

But Leola didn't talk again for a while. Then, finally, she spoke again. Her voice was quiet and Muffin knew she wasn't crying. "The last time he spoke to me, he said, 'Lee, I'm going out three, four hours and maybe

25

make a little money. Hard to make money Christmas cause people stay close to home and don't do much moving around.' And I said, 'Marvin, how come you can't stay close to home like other people? You don't need to drive no cab tonight. We ain't that hard up for money. Marvina and me want you here with us.' I said, 'You had a good dinner. How come you just can't relax and act lazy like everybody do on Christmas night?' And he said—remember what he said, Marvina?—he said, 'Maybe somebody out there need a good warm cab to ride home in.' He was putting on the new slippers you made for him. 'I'll drive in these tonight,' he said, 'and fool myself I'm home.' And then he kissed you and said, 'Come on, Lee, kiss me so's I can go.' And you remember, Marvina—I wouldn't do it cause I was mad. Remember he was standing in the doorway and he said, 'That's okay, Lee, I'll get it when I come back.' And he left." Muffin, her head deep into the pillow, turned away from her mother. And in the delicate quiet of the room Muffin heard her own breathing into the pillow, smelled dried and ironed Clorox. "Sometimes it sound like Marvin walking up the stairs coming home," she heard her mother say, crying, "and I have to open the door. When I tell the doctors that—they say they understand, but they don't. Don't nobody understand how it was with Marvin and me."

Muffin got up from the bed and went into the kitchen and opened the refrigerator and reached for the bottle of rum Mr. Dale had left in there last week. She took a tall glass from the cabinet and poured a lot of rum in it and a little Pepsi and put in ice cubes and went back to her room and handed the drink to her mother.

"What's that?"

"Some of Mr. Dale's rum and some Pepsi Cola, so you can go to sleep faster."

"You drink it."

Muffin sat down on the worn chenille bedspread and didn't know what to do, wanting to do something, wishing herself far away where the fire escape stars had gone, thinking tomorrow will come and tomorrow's today and Christmas will come and all this will be over with.

"You drink it. You drink it and be glad you blind—I wish I was blind, that's what I wish. I wish I couldn't see nothing."

The drink in Muffin's hand felt as if it had entered her body through her fingers and was filling her up. Drowning her and nobody could tell, nobody could see.

"Don't go no dance the day your father was murdered. Don't you go, Marvina. If that damn museum was so Black for real and lighting candles for Africa and all that stuff, they'd light a candle for your father. It was Black people he loved so much killed him."

When the alarm rang later that morning Muffin got up quickly and turned it off and went into her mother's room and listened to her loud breathing for a few moments and then turned the thermostat up to get rid of the morning cold. But when she reached down to pull up the corduroy comforter from the foot of the wooden double bed marked with bites from her baby teeth, she found her mother's thin arms locked tightly about a metal-framed portrait of her father. Muffin removed the picture carefully, without disturbing her mother's loud snores.

The warm metal was not life and did not remind Muffin of her father, and she put the picture coldly back in its place on the dresser, and thought only that her mother would sleep most of the day and maybe not drink and be drunk as she had been yesterday when Muffin came home from school.

Today was Tuesday. Last school day before the holiday break, and she, Muffin, was thankful. Maybe I can keep Momma from drinking so much, she thought to herself, if I'm home. Maybe things won't get so out of hand.

When Muffin had bathed and dressed and had run a pic quickly through her hair, she fried an egg and burned it and made it into a sandwich and ate it and drank a glass of buttermilk. She boiled two eggs and put them into a small saucer and placed it where her mother always sat. Then she went back to her room and sat down at her desk, moved aside the portable sewing machine, and took her stylus and paper and began to punch out a grocery list on the small, three-by-five index-card-shaped slate. Then she jumped up too quickly so that she disturbed her balance and had to wait carefully for a moment before she ran back to the kitchen. She pulled open the top drawer of the utility cabinet to the left of the sink and reached in and took out a handful of the thick plastic strips she used over and over again to mark canned goods. Then she went back to her room and sat back down at the desk and stuffed them into a small envelope and stuck the envelope down in her shoulder bag. She started punching out the grocery list on the small slate again.

Today she'd buy the turkey. She would buy it after school, when she bought the rest of the Christmas groceries.

"*We ain't having no Christmas dinner and all that mess, you hear me!*"

"*This is for Kwanza too, Momma.*"

"*We not doing nothing, Marvina—not for no Kwanza, not for no candles, not for no Africa; nothing. When Christmas come we just going to sit! You and me. And don't invite no company—not that boy either, ain't nobody coming in here.*"

Muffin punched out a few other things her mother had said they wouldn't have. For one thing, presents.

She had already crocheted the gifts she would give to Mr. Dale and Miss Geneva and Mr. Willie Williams and Mr. Osahar, her blind Black math teacher. And Ernie. The only presents left to buy were the ones her mother would give—even if she didn't want to.

And the most difficult of all, her gift to her mother. It had to be special. A very special thing. As special as the Kwanza dress.

Her first long, to the floor, dress. A taffeta jumper she had five days left to make—if she counted today and sewed all the way through Christmas Day. She had no idea at all of the kind of body blouse she'd wear with it. But the blouse wasn't important and neither were the shoes. The main thing was the jumper.

Mr. Dale would cut it out—but she, Muffin, would sew it. With all her heart she would sew it.

Muffin opened the dome of her watch and read seven fifty-five and got up from the desk and opened the closet and took out her pea jacket and put it on and buttoned it up. I'm not waiting for Ernie, she said to herself. I just want to be with me this morning. Me and the subway. Listening to each other scream through the dark. Yelling, I guess. But going on.

Muffin opened her sock drawer and reached under the paper and took out her mother's check and put it in the special lining she had sewn into her shoulder bag. Her mother had insisted she make the special pocket, always saying people would rob her. But people didn't hurt her, they helped her. Sometimes they helped too much and she'd get confused for a moment and lose her balance. Before, when she'd rocked a little, she'd never lost her balance. But the Black therapist had made her think to stop the rocking. Sometimes it was hard not to do it. It was easier too, to think when she rocked. Maybe if she rocked back and forth, she could chase away the Christmas sadness and make Kwanza come faster.

Five days until Kwanza. Five days to make her mother understand how much she wanted to go. Not to dance— she didn't care about dancing, she didn't know how to dance. Dancing was not important in her life. Except if she was dancing with Ernie. What was important, what she needed, was to be there on Christmas night, at twelve midnight when the first candle was lit—the first candle of her first Kwanza.

She didn't have to see it.

30

She just wanted to be there at the Black Museum, to be apart from her house and apart from her mother's crying, the smell of whisky, away from bottles. It didn't matter that she wouldn't look pretty in her long dress—she just wasn't pretty, but people would know she looked nice even if she was too tall and skinny and everybody knew about the way her mother acted. Nothing would matter except she was going to be there and Ernie was going to be there.

Daddy was the one who took me to the Black Museum when it first opened up, Muffin reminded herself. She took her dark glasses from the felt elephant and put them on and then unhooked her cane from the wooden pineapple. He wants me to go.

I just know it.

THREE

"I THOUGHT I'D GO CRAZY keeping my eyes open in school today. I think I fell asleep a million times —through the parties and everything! But I'm trying not to worry, Ernie," Muffin said quickly, leaning against the cold thick glass of a refrigerated meat case. "Even though Momma's drinking a lot. I mean she's drinking too much I think."

The boy said nothing, but kept watching the girl. Looking at the way she was talking more to the air than to him. He finished arranging lamb chops on a foil-covered shallow tray, placed it to the left of cubed beef, and closed the chrome and glass door near her. Then he got a broom, sprinkled sawdust, and began to sweep behind the counter. He had swept almost the entire floor before Muffin noticed he hadn't answered her. "What do you think, Ernie?" she asked, suddenly turning toward the heavy dust-laden darkness in front of him, seeing him clearly in her mind. Big, quiet, smooth skin, heavy mustache Ernie. Thick, high Afro. Most of it gray, people said, premature gray. "Ernie *real* fine,"

Deeta had said, "but he don't talk, just stares at people. Act too conceited for me."

"What you think, Ernie?" Muffin asked again, holding the dustpan for him and feeling the bits of dust enter her nose, her throat. Cling there.

"Stick with her," Ernie said.

"Stick with her!" Muffin cried and rubbed her nose against the arm of her pea jacket but lowered her voice when she heard a man come into the Earl 4X Market, roll a coin across the Formica counter toward Ernie, and pick up a copy of *Muhammad Speaks* from a stack by the door. Muffin knew which paper it was—only one was sold in the store. She started talking again as soon as the man left, the slammed door jarring her nerves, disturbing a balance in the air, creating an icy draft chilling her legs. "Okay, Ernie! That's what you say—'Stick with her.' But I stuck with her last night, and all this morning—real early, the best I could and everything was still a mess. I *do* stick with her. But what do I do after that? I mean if I help her get over this Christmas, the rest of the Christmases will all be right—it's just this one! I don't know how I'm going to the Kwanza, with Momma doing like this, acting like this."

"Doing what?"

"Everything!"

"No," Ernie said, his voice quiet as always. "She couldn't do everything."

Muffin sighed loudly. Ernie could certainly get on her nerves sometimes. Either he wasn't talking at all or he was being too specific. Like now, he was being too spe-   33 cific. Sometimes she thought he practiced up for when he was going to be a lawyer.

Okay. She would be specific too.

"First," Muffin said, "she didn't take her medicine and you know how she gets when she doesn't take it—you never know how she's going to act. Yesterday she was excited. Soon as I came home from school, I saw she was doing a whole lot of talking and asking for her check over and over again. And you know I had planned to go over what to buy for food—extra for Christmas—with her, trying to get whatever she wanted because when she buys she just buys everything and it costs too much and it never works out right. Because you know my father did all the shopping and made me find the stuff and figure out what we needed and everything like that. Momma never did it, only thing she did is cooked whatever we bought. So when I got home from school and saw how she was, I put the check, I've had it since Saturday, back in my drawer. And early this morning, while she was sleeping, I figured out what to buy. I think a lot of people will come by and see us this Christmas and I want Momma to have all the stuff she needs so she won't feel bad if she doesn't have anything to offer people. But Momma talks so terrible to people when she's real high and I feel sorry for them. Mr. Dale is the only one she can't outtalk. So, like I said, when I came home she was cleaning out my father's closet again and putting it back exactly and saying she had some place to go and for me to go get her check so she can go!"

34   "None of that's new," Ernie said. "She does the

closet thing all the time and she talks about your father—all the time. And when you don't want to give her her check, you don't. She knows that."

"Ernie, Momma drinks and then she wants to go out and last night it was real cold—you know it was! When my father was alive, Momma didn't go no place at night and she didn't even want him to be out at night with the cab. But he just went."

The door opened then and Ernie didn't answer. Several people came in, and while Ernie was waiting on them, Muffin took out her raised-dots grocery list. She ran her fingers quickly back and forth across the items she had so carefully listed and began to take them from the shelves and load them on one end of the counter. She put one of the loaves of bread back and took a package of wheat rolls from the bakery shelf. Her mother loved wheat rolls.

For a while, because she was concentrating on her list and pressing her plastic strips across the tops of cans and punching out what each one was, Muffin forgot her mother and forgot the customers she knew were staring at her. It was easy to shop here because Ernie kept the shelves a certain way, on purpose, for her. She hardly ever had to ask questions now. She knew how to buy and what to buy and what the real bargains were—thanks to Ernie and her own common sense. Money was precious and important and had to be spent carefully.

The biggest part of the money would be for meat. Ernie didn't eat meat any more, but her mother had said, "Don't talk to me about something simple like that; you better get meat and don't be foolish, Marvina!

Whoever heard of never eating no meat! You getting simple as you can be. That boy say die, you die!"

Ernie had said celery soup was on sale and Muffin took down ten cans of it. It was her favorite and easiest way to make gravy—one can of celery soup, dumped in the pan, with one can of milk. She liked shopping at the Muslim market better than at the supermarket. Nobody knew her well at the supermarket—nobody to say celery soup was on sale—and there was never anybody to explain things when she was really mixed up.

Most of all she liked Ernie's market because her father had liked shopping at the small Black grocery. In fact, as much as he could, she remembered, he went to Black stores for everything. The cleaners, the fish market, the drugstore. He was always saying, "Give the money to the Black stores, give it to our own people, then you know you helping and you know you not giving your money to the white all the time."

But her father had been killed, beaten to death by two Black men. His head was crushed by lead pipes held by Black men and nobody had found them yet, and people said if it had been a white cabdriver they would have found the killers right away. But finding the killers wouldn't make her father alive. She was never going to be held close to the wide shoulders under the worn-out sleeveless sweater again. The patient and explaining voice was gone: "Touch it careful now and feel it good. Don't let it fool you."

She was never going to hear him say: "This one's Muffin-girl and that one's Lee. She think she a girl still too, can't do nothing but talk."

"I'm girl enough for you, Marvin Johnson!" her mother would answer each time. "What you say to that! And I ain't no spring chicken either!"

Her father was gone and things were different. Now when she needed a kind of father she had Mr. Willie Williams—her father's "growing-up buddy."

"He gone and got religious on me," her father had said once. "Taught me all the bad I know and now he wants to pray it out."

And she had Mr. Dale.

Next to her mother, Mr. Dale was the best—not counting Ernie.

She was going to marry Ernie as soon as he started being an urban lawyer for Black people who couldn't afford to pay much money and got cheated all the time. And she was going to be in court when he fought all his cases and she was going to make his office a real Black office—with a flag made from red and green and black cloth that *really* came from Africa. Maybe she'd be a lawyer too. They'd be the best lawyer team in the whole country and only take Black people for cases and when they got rich they'd stay in a Black neighborhood and make it fabulous. People would say, "The Braithwaites, the two lawyers married to each other, did it." And when the children came and grew up, they were going to be great lawyers too. And when Ernie was real real old and couldn't fight cases any more, they'd come to him with one big case nobody could win but him, and Ernie would be in bed and he'd lie there and he'd say to her, "Think we can do it?" And she'd say yes and then he'd take the great case and win it and when he left the courtroom everybody would be standing up, including the judge, and Ernie wouldn't look back and even though she wouldn't be able to see it, she would know.

Ernie was very special. She was going to marry him— even if he never said anything when she said that.

Ernie never talked much anyway. The only person who really talked to her was Mr. Dale.

Once he had called her Cleopatra, Black Queen of the Nile.

That was dumb. Queens weren't supposed to be too tall and too skinny and she was. But she liked to hear him call her all the things she didn't know about but which sounded so nice anyway.

But sometimes Mr. Dale was confusing. "Stand tall," he'd say. "Stretch those elegant limbs of yours, flow! You are woman!" And later he'd say, "Little clumsy whooping crane child, do you *never* listen to me! Look how you're sitting!" Well, she had too much to do to think about sitting with her legs just so and her neck following some kind of shoulder line or something and anyway she wasn't a child and she certainly wasn't a woman.

But she was always going to love Mr. Dale, no matter how mixed up he was about what she was. It didn't matter that Ernie hardly spoke to him; Ernie hardly spoke to anybody.

Muffin's pile of groceries took up the whole end of the back counter. She was waiting now for Ernie to put aside the heavy groceries he would deliver to her house later. "There it is," he said when her shopping cart was filled. "Your books are on top. And I like your pattern."

"Ernie! Who told you to peek at my pattern, Ernie! Why'd you do that! I just stopped after school and I got it, drove the saleslady crazy telling me what everything looked like—she doesn't care though, she likes me. You know the one, the Black lady that helps me pick out all the stuff Mr. Dale says I have to buy to make something. Only thing is, they didn't have any taffeta and counting today all I got left is five days to sew, plus find material and— Now you had to go peek at my pattern!"

"I didn't peek at your pattern."

"You did look at it!"

"I didn't look at it."

"How'd you know I had a pattern?"

"I know shapes too," he said. "Especially in a small, flat bag with the top open. So just keep quiet and give me some money."

"I want you to be surprised," Muffin said, taking out the money Mr. Willie Williams had counted into her hand and she had folded just so, moments before she came into the market. Her mother would sign the check later. When the first check had come, her mother had refused to sign it and said she didn't want "dead husband money." And Mr. Willie Williams, Reverend Willie Williams, had just said to her, "Muff, bring the check around here to the church and I'll cash it. Then do what you have to do and let your mother know you're doing it. Save much as you can."

"Give your mother breathing room," Ernie was saying, closing the cash drawer.

"You just don't know, Ernie—maybe because it's not your mother. And all you can say is stick with her and don't crowd and all that breathing business and that's all you have to say. But what I have to say is I want Christmas to be over because I'm really scared for my mother with all this drinking and I'm scared for me."

Muffin scraped her cane across the wooden planks of the floor and then suddenly lifted the cane and ran her fingers lightly over the deeply cut-in names and the store was quiet and nobody was there but her and Ernie and she was in the dark and the dark was filled with the touch of carefully painted scratches.

"Things wouldn't be so bad, Ernie, if I could see and I'm not sad about it because I do all right and everybody helps me and you help me and you write on my cane and repaint it for me but it's still a cane. It's just a thing to keep me from getting hurt because I can't see, and that's what I mean about Momma. She's just the way she is and nothing's going to help her when Christmases come and so I want this Christmas to be over with. I mean when my father was alive, I didn't care too much about I couldn't see but with him gone and Momma going out in the street all the time—real late, I just wish I could see." The cane tip was quiet against her shoe, and the handle, hooked now over her wrist, felt silent too. "I wish I could make her happy but I just can't." Muffin thought then of the darkness that she took for granted, and sometimes feared. Things were hard a lot, too, for her. "People think I can do everything but I really can't, I really can't, Ernie!"

Don't talk, Muffin suddenly told herself. *Shut up!* Ernie can't help things, nobody could. And it was time to fix dinner. *Hook the cane over the cart handle and go. Push the cart and you don't need a cane.*

"Ernie," Muffin said at the door. "If something happens to Momma, I won't have anybody." Muffin felt the cart handle warm under her hands, and she moved them to another spot where it was cold. It felt good. "I thought about it last night when Mr. Dale had a hard time with Momma and when he can't help, it's really a mess. Mr. Willie Williams couldn't do much. Momma talked all over him saying, 'Don't be trying to act like Jesus when you and Marvina stealing my money.' But still Mr. Willie Williams tried to help and the whole time Momma was talking terrible to him! If it wasn't for Mr. Dale last night, I'd be nuts!"

Muffin realized Ernie was being too quiet, had stopped moving, but she didn't care. If she could, she'd scream louder than she was yelling now. Ernie could stand there and be as quiet as he wanted.

She snatched the door open but Ernie closed it. "What are you looking at me like that for!" she said and felt the words bounce against the ceiling and fall about her.

But Muffin didn't want to fuss. She didn't want to fuss at all, suddenly. Not with Ernie.

Except sometimes he just didn't *understand* things.

"Can you make it home okay?"

"Yes, I can make it home okay and I can make it okay period!"

Muffin heard Ernie move closer to her, could hear his shoes on the sawdust-strewn floor, felt him touch her hands. "Where're your gloves?" he asked softly.

"My hands aren't cold! Do my hands feel cold to you?"

"I don't know," he answered.

"Ernie, will you please move away from the door— *please!*" Why was she yelling at him?

Ernie leaned close and made a quiet kissing sound near her lips but he did not kiss her.

"I don't want anybody's kisses, don't kiss me!" That wasn't what she wanted to say either.

"I didn't kiss you."

"Ernie, move! Get your hands off the cart and let me open the door please, I have to go cook dinner and I'm already late and God only knows what Momma's doing!" Why did Ernie smell so good? Like a wet forest in a summer rain. One summer Ernie had driven her up to Seven Lakes and in a way she could almost see the narrow, winding country roads he had described for her. But it had started to rain and she liked rain and she had asked him to stop and he had and they had found a bench under a log shelter. And she had sat there listening to the light touch of water against natural things. But what she remembered most of all was the quiet of him. The rough embroidered designs on his African shirt. And the sweet smell of wet wood and wet grass and wet flowers.

42

Why was she remembering now? Summers like that were never now. Summers like that would never come again.

"*Asalaam Alaikum,*" Ernie said and opened the door for her and pulled the cart out to the sidewalk.

Wa Alaikum Salaam, Muffin wanted to answer but couldn't. "I don't know what peace is," she said to him.

But before she got to her corner and turned she whispered to the icy air, "Peace, Ernie. *Wa Alaikum Salaam.*"

There was little peace for her.

Peace was some fragile thing. It had to do with whether or not her mother had taken pills, could sleep, was high. Peace meant Mr. Willie Williams didn't mention God in her house. Peace meant Mr. Dale. Or it meant no peace at all maybe if he wasn't around.

Asalaam Alaikum, Muffin thought and walked into the vestibule of her apartment house, if Momma's okay when I get upstairs. She opened the heavy glass door and kept it from banging back against the aluminum cart. The hinge was broken and the door swung too fast but Muffin felt safe with that. The door always did the same thing.

"Hi, lady."

"Hi, Tank," Muffin said, walking backward and bumping the cart up the steps. The cane, still hooked onto the handle, thumped too.

Tank in the hall. Something you could expect. Could almost depend on. Like a door that swings open too fast.

Or like the door upstairs, next to Mr. Dale's, opening now. And Mr. Thomas looking out all day at people and never saying anything and his house smelling funny when he opened it and you were standing at Mr. Dale's. Mr. Dale saying Mr. Thomas was an old man. "How come he keeps opening his door and peeking out?" she had asked her mother.

"He's simple," she had said. "Some people just simple."

"I sure wish he didn't live next door to Mr. Dale. Almost every time I knock on Mr. Dale's door, Mr. Thomas opens his!"

"I told you he simple! What you worrying about him peeking out the door? This supposed to be a free country. If he want to look, he can look. People got a right to be simple! Say hello and keep getting up."

"I don't see how Mr. Dale can stand it!"

"Dale simple too," her mother had said, and then her tone changed. Muffin knew what was coming. "And when they get somebody not simple, they kill him—bash his head in till it don't look like a head. Cops standing around asking questions like they ain't got no sense either."

Cabbage and ham cooking.

Her mother was cooking dinner for the first time in two weeks.

"Marvina!" Leola called to Muffin, pulling the cart down the hall toward the kitchen. Then her mother met her halfway and hugged her hard and kissed her and unhooked the cane and threw it in on Muffin's bed and pulled the cart the rest of the way, her arm about Muffin's waist. "Look, see," she said, "you don't have to fix no dinner tonight, I did it. I didn't drink nothing today—I ain't drinking nothing no more and be simple. And I didn't need none of that medicine with all that cut-up tape you got on it so you know what it is. I been right all day, didn't mess up at all. All I was doing today was thinking. And we have to hurry up so we can eat. Cause you and me going somewhere." She kissed Muffin again. "Momma's glad you took the check the way you do when I act simple, and shopped. And I know you did everything right the way you always do and now you have to tell me what's left so we'll know how much to spend."

"Spend for what, Momma?"

"Spend for the best Christmas we can get. The kind Marvin would had. We doing it, Marvina. Just the way he want it!"

FOUR

"I THOUGHT YOU SAID you weren't going to celebrate Christmas or have anything to do with Kwanza," Muffin said, unable to really concentrate on putting the groceries in the right places, trying hard to hold back the joyous feeling that was beginning to swell within her. She listened for the usual signs and messages of trouble and couldn't read them, couldn't find them. Neither her mother's movements nor her voice were brittle—were sad. No sweet-sour smell of whisky. No irritable, jerky pill-caused sounds. No fuzzy, muffled pill words.

Her mother sounded good. Steady. And it was another change and Muffin liked it, wanted to hold onto it. Her joy rising higher. Pulling.

"I'm not celebrating nobody's nothing. I just feel like I want a tree and I been feeling funny about it all day, like Marvin in here making me feel this way. So it came to me to get a tree and decorate it with all the stuff—the way he like. With pieces of fruit cake on it. I didn't mess with no fruit cake this year because that was something he liked to do. Drown it in rum all year. So we first have to buy a plain old piece of fruit cake at the store and we won't eat it—just wrap foil on it and tie ribbon around it and hang it on the tree. What you think, Marvina?"

But Muffin didn't answer, couldn't answer. Not then, not for a while. Not while her mind was racing ahead making plans.

The joy thing inside was bursting and she didn't want to hold back any more, didn't want to question. But she had to, she had to. *Christmas and Kwanza and everything! Everything's working out!* Hold on. Hold tight!

No! Let it come.

And Muffin felt the flow, felt it in the dull flat paper wrapped around the can of peas and carrots she held in her hand.

Corn here, stringbeans there, baked beans in front. *Oh, Daddy, thank you, thank you!* Stack the new box of cookies behind the opened one. Sing! An empty raisin box. Remove it.

"Then you know what else, Marvina, sugar. Then we have to go buy something else tonight besides the tree. You and me can figure out the money. Two things more I want.

Eggs don't go in cupboards. Where's the refrigerator?

"I want me one of them big hi-fi sets he used to say he was going to make some extra money and buy. With a television. Everything."

Oh, no!

"Then we have to find all the Duke Ellington we can find."

"We can't buy a whole lot of stuff, Momma." Don't talk, Muffin said to her brain. *Listen.* "We can't afford it."

"Marvin and me used to love us some Duke Ellington!"

FIVE

Two hours later, in the Black department store, her mother was out of control. And for Muffin, joy was cut off. Gone.

"We don't need a stereo big as that, Momma," Muffin said, trying to keep her voice calm and hearing her mother's too-quick-to-answer voice get louder by the moment.

"This the one we getting, Marvina! This one just like what Marvin like—a whole lot of parts he can mess with. That's what he like, you know that. Messing, messing, messing—taking stuff apart just so he can see inside and then what he say—say, 'Lee-baby, watch this thing here.' And then if I look and don't see nothing, he say 'How's that? You see that?' And I say, 'Marvin, I don't see nothing.' And then he say, 'How come you can look, Lee, and not see what I'm showing you? The thing is clear as day.' And I'd say, 'So what if I can't see it, I can't see it! What it mean?' And he'd say, say, 'Lee—it don't mean nothing. It don't mean nothing if you can't see it.' "

"You have one on sale?" Muffin asked the salesman,

hoping he'd talk and stop just listening to them so much, not stand so quiet, his silver bracelets jangling. Crowded silver sound.

"We don't want nothing on sale," Leola said before the saleman could answer. "The thing we got now is a piece a junk not fit for nobody. Every time it's on five minutes, I got to get the needle from sliding cross. The thing either rejecting or sliding cross. Sliding, sliding—just the way she do with that cane! Long time ago, Marvin say, 'Lee, we need us a new box. Muffin got this thing so messed up we can't do nothing but give it to her to play with. Look how she got the thing doing.' But he always fixed it up and now don't nothing get fixed. You remember, Marvina. Tell me you don't remember your father saying a long time how we needed a new record player."

"But this one's got a television and we already have a nice TV! We don't need all this stuff, tapes and stuff, and even curtains on it!"

"It ain't got no curtains on it!"

"I feel them, Momma," Muffin said and tried to pull her mother's hand to the knotted, heavy, open-weave fabric behind the metal and wooden grill. "It feels like a mess to me!"

"Mess or not, we getting it."

Muffin wanted to yell but she was too tired; she wanted to go home. More than anything she wanted to go home. Wanted to get away from staring, whispering people. She knew they were staring, felt it through her bones, through muscle, through tissue. *Scream once.*

You're blind, you can't see. People will allow you to scream. Scream once. Scream loud. Scream!

But she didn't scream. Her voice when she spoke was soft, was quiet. "We can't afford it, Momma," she said.

"I know what we can afford and what we can't! You think I'm standing up here trying to buy something I can't afford, can't pay for!" Her mother's voice was rising again. "We want it," Leola said to the salesman that Muffin thought she felt touching her arm. Did she feel it? For a moment she thought she hadn't. But she had. There it was again. His silver bangles jingled. The salesman had patted her arm. *Take the cane and knock him away!*

"Please don't buy it, Momma."

"Hurry up, damn it, mister!" Leola said, more to Muffin than to the salesman. "Let me sign what I got to sign and go home and talk some sense in my child who thinks she the mother. She's not the mother, I'm the mother!"

"So, you're going to do it, Momma," Muffin said angrily, shaking off the gentle, now too noisy and too close, hand touching hers. Right then she wanted to take her cane and knock everything away from her the way she used to do. Then knock the cane away too. But that was before. Before when she was ten and safe. "You really mean you're going to get that thing when you know we don't have the money. When you *know* we don't have the money! We don't have an extra twenty dollars a month to pay for something we don't

51

need and this thing feels like it's going to cost fifty. It feels like it'll cost a hundred a month!"

"And I told you all day I been thinking on it and I remember how last year your father said he was going to get us a new one—a new record player. That's what he was working round the clock for. Trying to get the things he thought maybe we want!"

"Daddy wouldn't have bought anything as expensive as that—just walk in and buy it, and you know it!"

"Now how you know what to do! He didn't never talk to you about no hi-fi!"

"He wouldn't buy anything feeling like that! All you're paying for is all the extra wood and we don't have fancy furniture like that and we don't need to either! Daddy wouldn't want us to spend money on a lot of dumb stuff we can't afford!"

"Maybe you want to wait until he can come in and take a look at it," the salesman said.

"My father's dead," Muffin said. "He died last year on Christmas Day!" Deal with that, Muffin thought and wanted to laugh. Deal with that! But she really wasn't angry at the young salesman. She knew he was young. He wasn't even acting like he wanted to sell the set. Most of all he was listening, saying nothing.

His bracelets were still. Nobody was saying anything.

Then Leola spoke. "He didn't do no dying. He was beat to death and bled to death and cops stood around and didn't do a damn thing! You Black," she said to the salesman, "you know how it is. She's young and don't know from nothing and she's blind, you can see she's blind. What I wish is she had my eyes and she can take mine. I don't want to see nothing no time, no more."

"Let's go, Momma," Muffin said and walked away a little.

Her mother didn't follow.

"We getting it, Marvina. We can figure out the money later but this the one I want. You can't see how it look. I can see how it look and it look like Marvin."

"Hope you don't need it for six weeks," the salesman said. "Cause there's none in the warehouse."

Thank the Great Black Almighty God in Heaven!

"But since you already signed everything—and it's Christmas—I'll give you the floor sample of a good stereo and it's small enough for you to take home with you tonight. I'll throw in an album free. On the house."

Muffin didn't breathe until her mother answered.

"You got Duke Ellington for free?"

"I got one for you," he said.

Later, while Muffin heard the box being turned around and around and cord stretched tight about it and while her mother was fussing with the albums sales-man, she felt the jangling bracelets close to her. "Let me know," he said, "what you want to do. We have close to twenty of those curtain monsters in the ware-house right now. Take my card. Call me if you can get her to keep the one she's taking tonight—it's good equipment. I'll change the figures on the papers—you don't have to come back in." He handed Muffin the small card and told her his name. "Just call."

Muffin wanted to hug him but all she managed to do was whisper, "Thank you very much."

"Forget it," he said. "Be good to her and try to call me before the week's out."

The cold Brooklyn air didn't seem so cold to Muffin, and the double-handled box she and her mother were carrying together wasn't heavy. "You go on and do that tapping with that cane," her mother was saying. "I can carry this little piece a nothing! Ain't good as the one we got!"

Muffin listened to her mother's voice and the sound of her cane touching the sidewalk, and felt her joy come back. Happiness poured in again.

She felt glad that she had a new stereo and she couldn't understand the new sudden feeling about being happy about the thing. When a cab finally stopped for them, they got in and she forgot about trying to understand. She wished she had said something better than thank you to the salesman. Daddy's right, she thought, squeezed against the box in the back of the cab. Black stores treat you the best.

"Marvin see that pretty box—the one coming later," her mother was saying. "He be messing around with it all day Christmas—or what you call it. Kwanza. What you say—Merry Kwanza? What you say?"

"Happy Kwanza."

When the cab stopped, somebody was opening the door on her mother's side and reaching in and taking the box from them. Muffin knew exactly who it was.

Leather jacket creaking. The smell of wet wood and wet grass and a wet forest in a summer rain.

"I brought your food around three times," Ernie said, and kissed her mother. "How you doing, Mrs.

Johnson?" he asked laughing, a quiet Ernie-laugh. "Tell me how you doing."

"Don't be kissing me," Muffin heard her mother say. "You don't know nothing about kissing. Only person like your kissing is Marvina and she don't know nothing either."

But an hour later, while Ernie was connecting the speakers, Leola Johnson was rubbing and patting his back.

Everything's going to be all right, Muffin thought, sitting in the plastic-covered wing-back living room chair, feeling happy, listening to her mother—mostly her mother—and Ernie talking.

The very best thing of all is for Momma to be making this Christmas just like Daddy was here.

It's perfect.

SIX

"You just a work-hard young man,"
Leola was saying. "A plain old work-hard young man.
Got more gray hair in your head than me. You better
slow down take it easy." Muffin heard her snatch something from Ernie. "You hear me!"

"Okay," Ernie said.

"Now, don't say no okay and keep messing with that
record player. Turn around here. Look at me."

Ernie, still on the floor, twisted around. Leather
jacket screeching a bit.

"Momma, will you calm down a little," Muffin
begged.

"Here she go, first thing she think about is calm
down, Momma—sleep, Momma. Don't cry, Momma.
Later for that! I want to cry, I cry. I want to sleep,
I sleep. I want to get blue, I just get blue. Marvina
do what she want, I do what I want. Hurry up," she
said to Ernie, "put the Duke on. He do what he want
too!"

"Which side you want?" Ernie asked.

"Every side," her mother answered. "The Duke got plenty sides."

While Muffin was putting away groceries for the second time that day, listening to the too-sudden stillness in the living room and the moaning piano and horns of what Ernie told her was "Blues To Be There," she heard her mother say, "I got to go."

Muffin got down from the stool and tried not to act alarmed when she got to the living room. "Say the word and you got a chauffeur," Ernie was saying.

"Momma, where are you going?"

"I'm going where I'm going!"

"Ernie?" Muffin said carefully. "Can you take Momma where she wants and wait since it's so cold out?"

"No, he ain't!" Leola said, before Ernie could answer. "He can't take me where I'm going. He can take you where you going but he can't take me where I'm going!"

"I don't mind," Ernie said. "Where you want to go?"

"None of your business. How's that!" Leola said, checking windows to make sure they were locked.

Pictures and sounds were bumping into each other somewhere inside Muffin, mixed with the clacking of venetian blinds snapping up and down.

Everything was split up but her mother's plans. The hopes she had didn't matter. The only things that counted, the only ideas to be followed, were her mother's.

And her mother didn't really care about Christmas, didn't really care about making things nice to be reminded of Daddy, didn't care about her. She's going out, Muffin heard herself yelling. She's going out to drink whisky and spoil everything. She's going out to get drunk.

"You two just children, don't be checking on my time. Marvina think cause she so tall, she the mother. She not the mother, I'm the mother!"

"No, Momma," Muffin said angrily, "I'm not the mother. But I'm big enough to know you don't have any place to go but the Midnight Club."

The room was very quiet and Muffin didn't care about the quiet and she didn't care about Ernie being there, couldn't see him, didn't know where he was in the room, couldn't hear him.

"Don't say nothing else, Marvina!"

"That's where you're going, Momma, even when you said at dinner you weren't going to drink anything else and you were going to make this a nice Christmas and everything. But if you go out and drink whisky I'm not giving you your medicine when you come in and I'm not going to sit up all night while you hug Daddy's picture either!" Muffin went over to the windows and unlocked them. "I'm not afraid of anything outside," she said. "The stuff that goes wrong goes wrong in here, so you can just unlock all the windows. Nobody's going to come in here bothering us. People just feel sorry for us and I hate it. I hate it!"

58   "You finished?"

"No, Momma. I just don't care no more. I do the best I can do and you just keep on doing anything you want. You don't listen to anybody."

Muffin felt her mother's thin hand hard against her face but it didn't hurt. And she wasn't embarrassed by Ernie's seeing it. Ernie could understand. She knew that.

Her mother was shouting. "I been cooking all day! You didn't cook today—when you got home from school you sat down and you ate. And I didn't take none of them simple-behind pills the doctors give me! Simple-ass pills make me so stupid I don't even know my name!"

"You got good doctors, Momma."

"I got my own way to help me. I don't like taking no whole lot of medicine."

"But when you drink that whisky," Muffin yelled, "all you do is beg me for your pills!"

"You don't give them to me do you?"

"No!"

"Well, then you ain't got no worries!"

"I'm leaving," Ernie said.

Muffin heard the door open, then close and Ernie's footsteps going down the stairs and away from her. All things went away from her. Her father, her mother, plans, hopes, Mr. Dale, Mr. Willie Williams—

"All that hollering mess. You embarrassed the boy!"

"I wish I could have left when he left!"

"Go on!"

"No, Momma. You're the only one around here able   59

to do whatever you want—when you want to, no matter what!"

"Being blind don't stop nothing!"

"I'm not talking about—Oh, Momma! Momma, do what you want."

"You yelling at me, Marvina!"

"No, Momma, I'm not yelling—I'm sorry. I'm not yelling."

"Well, act like you not yelling!"

Thirty minutes later her mother was gone and Muffin was knocking on the satiny, specially paneled door of Mr. Dale, and holding her hand over the peephole.

On her right, she heard Mr. Thomas open his door a little and she smelled that strong smell of dusty old things that always stayed in her nostrils even after the door was closed.

Muffin didn't look toward him but kept her fingers over the small cold brass disk.

When Mr. Dale opened his door, Muffin could hear Mr. Thomas walking down his own hall toward the kitchen, the sound of his footsteps, hollow. As if his rooms were bare. And she would have wondered, the way she always did, what he did all day besides open his door and peep out at people.

But she didn't have the time to wonder about it. Mr. Dale had opened the door and Muffin reached out to touch him and felt the soft robe she loved, the one he said was light brown cashmere. She liked to put it on, liked to wrap it close about her, liked the way the huge, deep fur collar tickled her face.

60

But he was fussing at her.

"My God!" He cried. "I've just massaged a warm honey pack into my face and I've got ice cubes in minted water to remove it and here you come to ruin it all!"

SEVEN

"How come you put honey on your face?" Muffin asked a few minutes later, while she leaned against the doorway of the bumpy-textured-tile bathroom.

"It helps me understand girls who wear linty corduroy bathrobes. I don't blame the buttons," he said, splashing the peppermint-smelling water all over his face and patting the skin rhythmically. "I'd leave too."

Muffin straightened up and touched the three pins holding the bathrobe she had pulled on hastily before she left and hoped he wouldn't notice the rapidly disintegrating foam bedroom slippers on her feet. She was scared to move her toes, afraid he'd see. How come he didn't understand bathrobes didn't last forever? He had taught her to sew, making this same one! Four years ago! "Well, you know how old it is," she said. "And I can't afford a new one with Momma trying to buy record players with televisions and tape decks and tape recorders attached to it!"

"When?"

"A little while ago—this evening!" Muffin said. "But

the salesman tricked her and told her they didn't have any more left and gave her a small one to take home that they used to demonstrate to people. Then he whispered to me to make her keep it and later on—before we left— he said he'd use the papers she signed for the other one. The big one. He said he'd change the figures."

"Good man."

"But Momma can still go back and get another sales- man or go by herself after the holidays and maybe the salesman will get in trouble."

"Leola needs a stereo like I need a hole in the head!"

"She said Daddy wanted one and she says we should get it and she wasn't going to drink no more and we were going to have the kind of Christmas Daddy would have. At first I was glad but then she went out tonight and I know she's going over to your bar and drink. And I wish in a way you didn't even have that bar across the street."

Mr. Dale walked past her and out the bathroom. Muffin followed behind him on the thick shag carpet, the long loops out of place against the ragged foam of her slippers.

"For God's sake, Muffin—walk!"

"I *am* walking!"

"You are *not* walking, you're tipping!"

"I don't want to mess up and mash down your carpet."

"Don't it feel good under your feet?"

"Yes," Muffin said. "Real soft and everything."

"Enjoy," Mr. Dale said. "Walk!"

Muffin wanted to laugh. She loved coming up, loved to hear him tease her, loved the sink-down-in huge   63 leather sofa—brown, he had said a dozen times: "Like everything else in here. Chocolate. Sweet, bittersweet chocolate! Beautiful!"

Muffin flopped down on the sofa. The leather wasn't stiff like Ernie's jacket nor did it have the raw smell.

"Come on back here," Mr. Dale called to her. "I'm sewing."

"Oooh!" Muffin cried, jumping up from the deep soft fine leather. The sewing room, to her, was the best place in the whole house.

Mr. Dale was already sitting down at the machine. "Eggshell colored silk," he said, handing her the material, placing it in her hands. "Pure silk! I love it to death!"

"Wow," Muffin said, though she didn't know a thing about pure silk, and handed it right back. "I won't bug you, I promise—I'll just watch and keep quiet." But instead of sitting on the long, inlaid leather, satiny wooden bench across from the machine, she was moving her hands along her favorite place. A wall-to-wall rack suspended from the ceiling.

Muffin knew every piece of material on the hangers. And she knew immediately when something was missing. And when there was a new piece, she'd discover it, often before he told her.

Muffin loved touching the fabrics hanging under plain plastic and in zippered plastic bags. Light colors on one end, he had said. Dark colors on the other. She knew the summer material, knew where the winter fabric hung. She touched the package of long leather strips.

And she touched what she knew to be his absolutely favorite piece. Pale pink suede, he had said.

"You *still* haven't made this into anything," she said. "How come you can't decide!"

"I got to get a feeling first."

"You don't say that with the rest of the stuff."

"*That* piece is not the rest of the stuff."

"I wish you'd make something out of it quick. I just can't wait no more. You should make another suede jumpsuit like the red one, the one with the boots to match."

"Oh, Jesus! I've a thousand things prettier than that jumpsuit."

Muffin sat down on the bench then, propped her elbows on her knees, and made a cradle for her face with her hands. But Mr. Dale got up from the machine and walked into his bedroom. "I thought you were going to sew the silk stuff," Muffin yelled after him.

"And I thought you said you wouldn't bug me!" he called back to her."

"Okay, okay."

Moments later, he was sitting back at the machine and Muffin could hear him putting the silk material aside and laying something heavier across the machine table. She heard him remove the bobbin case, click out a bobbin, click another in its place, and snap the little metal piece back into the machine. She could hear him snatch off one spool of thread and replace it with another and pull the thread through and around where it belonged. Then she heard him cutting the heavier material. Not with the heavy, dull-sounding pinking shears but with the sharp, precise dressmaker's shears.

"What you sewing now?" Muffin asked. "What are you doing? What color is it?"

"I'm cutting a delicious red satin band off a long red nylon and wool housecoat."

"Why're you taking the bottom off?"

"I'm not taking the bottom off, I'm taking off a band *at* the bottom!"

"How come?"

"Cause you're not ready for such a gorgeous piece of satin."

"You—you're taking it off for me? You're giving it to me?"

"That lint disease you wearing got terminal on you, baby."

"Ohhh!" Muffin cried and jumped over to him, pulling the material a bit from the needle.

"Jesus!"

"Oh, I'm sorry," Muffin said, touching the soft robe and stepping back. She sat down again quickly on the bench. "Can I have the band?" she asked.

"No. I'm cutting an inch off—you're not tall as me, then I'm using the band as a facing and I'll scallop. The satin will hide inside and feel good on your ankles and be safe from lint!"

Muffin reached forward and touched the soft red. "It's pretty."

"How you know it's pretty?"

"It feels pretty."

66   "How does pretty feel?"

"Like this," Muffin said, touching the robe again.

"Touch me," he said.

Muffin did.

"That's how pretty feels," he said.

Muffin was still laughing a little when he finally said, "Put it on. And leave that mess you wearing in the bathroom. I shall flush it."

"You can't flush a bathrobe," Muffin said.

"*That* one will flush."

Muffin went running to the bathroom and never once thought about mashing down the carpet. But in the bathroom, her old robe at her feet and the soft new one wrapped around her, she felt suddenly not happy. She reached down and picked up the crumpled cotton corduroy thing from the floor and folded it carefully.

She couldn't leave it here with Mr. Dale.

This was the same robe he had taught her how to sew with, her fingers moving slowly, fearfully. She had learned every part of the machine while making this very robe. Her father had bought the corduroy for her and each night she had tried to explain what she had learned and he had said to her, "That's good. I'm glad you can do it; listen to him. He knows about sewing." And when her father had come in one night with a sewing machine of her very own, she had used the same pattern to make a robe for her mother.

No. She couldn't let Mr. Dale throw it out. She would take it home and hang it in her closet. Not the way her mother hung her father's things and moved them around and put them back in the same place and talked about this shirt and that sweater and that jacket and this suit. She, Muffin, was just going to hang it up and that was going to be that.

Muffin put the folded cloth on the end of the huge sofa. And it felt fragile against the massive arm.

"Dynamite," Mr. Dale said when she walked back into the sewing room. Then he continued to sew again on the silk. Muffin listened to the steady drive of the machine's motor.

"Baby, baby, don't be quiet. Talk."

"Momma's drinking a lot of whisky."

The drive of the machine was steady, not disturbed.

"She says she's going to do something and then she—" It was hard to talk right now. Maybe it was the way the new robe felt. Or maybe it was Mr. Dale not paying her any attention. But what more could he do to help? He was already the best person when things were real bad. Except the stuff he told her to do, when her mother was acting up, never worked unless he was right there. "But I'm just not going to worry about it," she said, her words filling out the sound of the machine, fitting in. "I'm just going to not worry about Momma. I mean, at first, I thought maybe Momma would come with me to the Kwanza but now she says she won't come with me and Ernie. Ernie's even taking his sisters—I mean it's supposed to be for families and everything."

"What's Leola doing Christmas?" Mr. Dale asked. But Muffin was staring at the darkness and not watching him. She wasn't talking about Christmas, she was talking about *after* Christmas.

68

"I wanted her to go with me. A lot of people'll be

there and I wanted Momma to go. They're having Black poetry and music and singing and stuff and Etta Moten Barnett is coming and I like to hear her talk, her voice I mean. I mean all the words are perfect and the way she sounds, it sounds like she's a movie star on a stage—You ever hear her talk?"

"No," Mr. Dale said. "Is young Jesus running the Museum's Kwanza?"

"Ernie?" Muffin said and didn't laugh at all. "I don't think you should call Ernie that—Jesus, I mean. I'd be scared to say it."

"I thought he was almighty!"

"But you shouldn't *say* that!"

"Don't be frightened, sweet Kwanza baby. I understand that for you and for me, all the gods are Black now —even The Main One, Him. Though I suspect they're through with me—which is totally uncool."

Muffin knew Mr. Dale was smiling, but right then, for her, nothing was funny. "Momma'll probably still be at the Midnight Club when you get there tonight."

"Get into a happy! Jesus! Stop bugging yourself. Leola'll be all right tonight. Cause I'll be there taking care of business—*her* business—if she ain't!"

"As soon as Ernie fixed up the stereo—hooked the speakers and stuff to the wires, and put on that Duke Ellington album, Momma said she had to go."

Muffin heard Mr. Dale's always fast sewing, the machine motor driving rapidly, and she waited for him to say something and he didn't. Listening to the machine poured too much noise in her head. She wanted to go home. But she sat, staring into the dark.

"*Asalaam alaikum.*"

"*I don't know what peace is.*"

"Find a dress yet for your Kwanza?"

"Oh," Muffin said, sliding quickly off the bench and going back to the sofa. The dark forgotten. She felt around and couldn't find the pattern she had had in her hand when she first came up. She ran into the bathroom and reached up to the wide shelf laden with perfumes and lotions and creams.

The pattern was there, where she had placed it. Just before she had begun to swish her finger back and forth in the minty-smelling water Mr. Dale had used to ice his face seven times.

"You like it?" she asked, and stuck it in his face.

He kept sewing.

"You still want yellow?"

"Yeah!" But what was it she heard in his voice?

"Yeah?"

"I mean yes—" Muffin's heart threatened to stop beating and she could not sense what she was listening for most. She was about to move closer to him but instead moved to the left. Something was there, there to the left of him. Hanging up on the rack.

She touched it now just as she had touched it the first time, a year ago. There it was, in the plastic bag, crinkled tissue layered through the folds.

"*What is it?*"

"*Panne velvet.*"

"*What color?*"

"*Yellow.*"

70

"*Yellow—what kind of yellow?*"

"*Yellow like lemons.*"

Mr. Dale was quiet, and Muffin's heart had come to a full and seemingly complete stop. Her stomach was waiting for something.

"You got it," Mr. Dale said.

"Oooooh!" Muffin yelled and then yelled again and hugged him. The fur collar of his robe felt warm and soft against her face, her neck. She hugged him harder. "Oh, Mr. Dale!" she cried. "Oooh! I can't believe it, I just can't believe it. Thank you! Ooooooooooh!"

When Muffin finally pulled away from him and stopped yelling, she didn't even feel silly. How could you feel silly with six yards of lemon yellow panne velvet all your own? Muffin was still holding the zippered plastic bag against her when she asked, "You like my pattern?"

"It's horrible!"

Muffin's heart suddenly started beating again but her stomach gave way. "But the lady, you know the one you introduced me to—the Black saleslady that's always helping me with material—well, she told me how it looked and traced the lines on me around the neck! Only they didn't have taffeta—like Deeta said to get, and I wanted to get the blouse but I knew I couldn't do that until I got the taffeta and knew what color it would be and everything!"

"Ugh!"

"I didn't know what else to wear!"

"How did you come up with a jumper and blouse?"

"That's what Deeta's wearing!"

"Oh, Jesus, God Almighty," he cried.

71

"Well, she said—she said we should look alike."

"It's over!" he shrieked. "I can't teach you!" Mr. Dale sighed loudly then and Muffin knew she was supposed to understand something but she didn't know what it was.

"Cut the material in half," Mr. Dale was fussing. "You take half and give Deeta half and then the two of you will be exactly alike and I shall be certain then—positive, absolutely positive, that you've never learned a thing from me!"

"I know you'll have to cut it out for me," Muffin said, ignoring what he said, "because you always do and Momma can't cut out patterns. But, mainly will you make it for me? Make the dress?"

"No."

Muffin panicked. "I might make a bad mistake!"

"No."

"But, it's Tuesday and Kwanza is almost here—I mean it's Sunday. I mean it actually starts the minute December 26 comes, which is Christmas night! And I don't have enough time! I mean—the taffeta was okay but I might spoil *velvet!*"

"No."

"I'm scared to do it," Muffin cried, really frightened. "I might mess up and then it'll look a mess and the velvet will be ruined! Please, Mr. Dale, you have to make this one. I won't *ever* ask you to make anything else. I promise! I dee-double promise!"

"I'm going to sit here at this merciless machine and sew something just so you can look exactly like Deeta?"

"I mean then I don't need to wear a jumper and a blouse, I mean—maybe I can think of something else—

maybe another idea!" Muffin panicked again, styles were never clear in her mind.

"You make the dress."

"I'm scared!"

"I'm scared too!"

"Scared of what?"

"You and Deeta."

"Okay! I said I won't dress like her, I *said* I won't! I'm afraid to ruin it, to make a mess. I can't see!"

"You make a mess, you wear a mess."

Muffin sat down on the wooden bench for what seemed like the hundredth time.

He meant it.

She, Muffin Johnson, would have to make her own most important dress in the world. She was also going to have to find another pattern. She couldn't wear anything Mr. Dale called horrible. "You think I can really do it?" she asked very quietly.

Mr. Dale didn't answer.

Muffin got up and walked over to the long plastic bag. She touched it again. "It's mine now."

"It's yours."

"Your friend doesn't want it."

"I said it's yours."

Muffin squeezed the bag to her for the second time that night and then lifted it up and took it down from the rack.

If it was hers, she was taking it home.

"The pattern lady's going to have a fit when she sees me again," Muffin said, not really caring. Right then, all she cared about, in the world, was a zippered

73

plastic bag filled with lemon yellow panne velvet and tissue paper. "Mr. Dale," she said. "Remember when you said you'd put my hair in African plaits? Could you do it for me for Kwanza? Please?"

"You will have braids—woven with wooden beads—for your Kwanza."

Then Muffin went to Mr. Dale and hugged him hard and he let her and she could feel his smile, along with the fur against her cheek. And it came to her that if Ernie was the smell of wet wood and wet grass, a quiet forest in the rain, then Mr. Dale was some rare flower crushed and pressed and dried and treasured.

Maybe, later tonight, if she couldn't sleep and her mother was still out, she'd try to write how she felt about him on paper. Pressed out carefully with her stylus, maybe the poem would come.

But she had to let go of him now. Someone was banging on the door.

Muffin heard Mr. Dale's kidskin slippers slapping against his heels as he walked down the hall, heard him push aside the peephole lever.

"It's Leola," he said. "Looking simple."

"You the one looking simple," Muffin heard her mother say as soon as he had opened the door.

EIGHT

"AIN'T NOTHING MORE simple-looking than a grown-old-behind man, with gray hair, walking around in fur!"

"In mink, darling!"

"Feel sorry for the mink! Where my child? Where Marvina!"

Muffin, the plastic bag over her arm, walked into the living room where her mother was.

"Now here she come decked out in red. You two look like a circus—Marvina, how you going to wash dishes in that thing!"

"I can do it," Muffin said, listening carefully to her mother. Had she come back to get Mr. Dale? He always left to go to his Midnight Club at eleven thirty. It was almost eleven now.

Muffin heard her mother snapping her fingers to the music from Mr. Dale's never-turned-off stereo. She didn't sound as if she had had anything to drink. And she wasn't talking confused either. Except she's excited. *Momma's too excited.*

"She tall just like Marvin," Leola Johnson said, suddenly reaching up and kissing Muffin and temporarily crushing the yellow velvet. Faint smell of sour. Whisky. "Ain't she, Dale?"

"Um-hm," Mr. Dale answered.

"She standing up there looking like Marvin for the world, got that pretty dark skin and heavy eyebrows just like Marvin. He could wear red good too, just like her. I don't fit with them. They the best part of me—the best part of Leola. Marvin and Marvina!"

She was snapping her fingers again. "Keep on being quiet," she said close to Muffin's face. "It don't make me *no* never mind!"

Muffin could hear her dancing about on the beautiful shag carpet, mashing it without rhythm.

"Marvina," Leola said, laughing. "Be glad you can't see. This place look like a funeral parlor, drapes and all—same kind they put behind caskets!"

"Those curtains," Mr. Dale said, "are handmade, custom cut, Austrian puffs."

"Take it down and get yourself a little bit a Africa. Get some Africa curtains—and I bet they won't be looking like nothing they put for dead people. Ask Marvina, Marvina know about that Africa stuff."

"Let's go, Momma."

"Let's go, Momma. What that mean?"

"Leola," Mr. Dale said. "I got to get to the Midnight. Go home. I am putting you out!"

"What that mean?" her mother asked again and kept dancing. "You putting me out? I go when I want!"

Muffin stood, holding the plastic bag and wondered

what it was and why she was holding it. Suddenly, yellow panne velvet didn't make sense.

"Marvina think I been drinking but I ain't. Leola just feel good, I feel real good. And I got something for her downstairs—but she act so simple when I said I was going out, I shouldn't let her see. I call myself coming up here to get her, to show her—but all I get is her quiet act. That ain't no sign of nothing to me!"

"I'm ready to go home and see, Momma."

"Well, I ain't ready to show—how you like that!"

Muffin heard her mother hit Mr. Dale. "Dance with me," she said. "I feel like dancing."

Mr. Dale danced her to the door.

"I'm leaving cause I want to leave, cause I'm sick of you—that's why I'm going! Where my child! Where's Marvina?"

"I'm right behind you, Momma. I'm coming."

"Be careful walking down the steps. That simple-looking red thing you got on can trip you up, break your neck!"

Muffin heard Mr. Thomas open his door.

"Close it," her mother said to him. "Or else—say Merry Christmas. Say Merry Christmas or shut the door!"

Muffin didn't turn toward Mr. Thomas's door but she heard it close quietly.

"Peeping, peeping, peeping—don't say nothing! Just peep!"

Though Muffin couldn't see Mr. Dale in his doorway at the top of the stairs, she knew he looked perfect. The long, scalloped red robe she wore and the bunched-up bag of yellow velvet and tissue paper seemed to be still connected to him in some way and out of place with the old robe on her arm and her mother's voice.

Crude, in contrast to him.

It seemed to fit when he called after her, "Your pretty red is dragging the steps, sweet Black plum!"

"You dragging too," her mother called back. "You dragging—steps or not!"

"Good*night*, Leola! And Muffin, there *is* a way to walk in a long garment and I shall have to teach you!"

"He going to teach you how to walk down some damn steps," Leola said when Mr. Dale had closed the door. "That got to be a joke. He trying to learn how to walk down them his ownself! But I ain't thinking about Dale —you wait till you see what we got!"

Muffin smelled it as soon as her mother opened the door.

A Christmas tree.

"You and me and Marvin going to have us a real Christmas."

Muffin went to the tree and touched it, still clutching the plastic bag and her old robe.

"Take that mess out your hand and feel it. Touch it all over. You like it?"

"Yes," Muffin answered. She really did. It was tall and scrawny but it was a real Christmas tree and it made things smell good and her mother was happy. She had been drinking, but not badly.

Not like last night.

"What's that mess you holding so tight?"

"Mr. Dale gave me some material."

"Why you want all the stuff he got!"

"He just gave it to me, Momma—he gives me material all the time. This is enough for a dress and if we go to Kwanza, I can wear it."

"We celebrating here in the house. Go and make the dress, make it for Christmas here in the house. And I'm not going to upset myself talking about it tonight cause I don't want you mad at me, your lips poking the ground. I'm trying to give you a nice Christmas, best anybody can have with a father murdered on Christmas Day. I got a lot of plans—all we have to do is talk money. But you just like Marvin, could make a dollar holler to get out his hand." Leola tried to take the plastic bag from Muffin but the girl held tight. Her mother patted her back. "You do good with money, I ain't complaining. You do everything just right like your father and I'm real proud cause you can do more blind as a bat than a whole person."

"I am a whole person, Momma."

"Well, I ain't!"

Her mother was still talking when Muffin walked back into her room and pulled off the soft robe and laid it across the foot of the bed and hung the old one in the closet and sat down on the bed. She unzipped the plastic bag and took the velvet out and moved her hand over the slick finish and then against the nap and then smoothed it again. She put her fingers under and felt the fabric cling, take the shape of her hand, drip over it.

"Marvina! Come let's fix the tree!"

"It's late, Momma."

"Let's decorate a little bit!"

"No, Momma."

"You mad cause I had a little drink, you smell things like a damn bloodhound. Okay, don't help me!" her mother called while Muffin was hanging up the plastic bag. "I'll do it myself. Me and Marvin! All I want you to do is come find that old stand for the tree and that sheet you sewed at the blind camp."

By the time the tree was standing firmly upright in the rusty metal stand and the embroidered sheet draped perfectly about its base, Muffin flipped open her watch and read one twenty-one.

Wednesday. Four more days until Kwanza. Suppose I can't find a pattern tomorrow, she thought, though she was too tired to panic.

"I got it made now," her mother said. "Go way."

"Momma, please go to sleep and get some rest. We can decorate tomorrow."

"Tomorrow ain't no sign of nothing!"

Muffin heard her reach for and pick up and drink from the glass she kept putting down on the glass-centered coffee table. "Don't help me do nothing. I bought the damn tree didn't I? Well, if I bought it, I can decorate it!"

Five minutes later Muffin took her mother's pills out of the bathroom cabinet and out of the kitchen cabinet and out of the top drawer of her bureau in her room and from under the mattress in her room and unzipped the plastic bag with the lemon yellow panne velvet in it and stuck the bottles and vials in a bunch of tissue paper at the bottom. Then she pulled the material a little forward and hoped none of the bottles could be seen.

Then she touched the plastic bag and it didn't seem real that the lemon yellow panne velvet she had loved for a year was actually hanging in her closet, and she put her face against the heavy plastic covering, for a moment.

But Muffin was in bed, snuggled against the pillow, when she heard her mother mumble, "Watch and see don't I decorate this tree tonight! Me and Marvin."

NINE

"YOU LIKE THIS PATTERN, ERNIE? I just bought it and I'm showing it to you—and not surprising you—because I want you to look at it and tell me if it'll look good in yellow panne velvet. It's a wrap-around dress and I'll probably still be sewing right up till midnight Christmas when Kwanza comes in. You like it?"

Ernie didn't answer.

Muffin snatched the pattern off the counter and did the best she could to glare in Ernie's direction. Ernie had been acting dumb ever since she had come by that morning—before she had gone shopping for the pattern—and said that she was definitely going to the Kwanza, and since she had said Mr. Dale had given her the yellow velvet, and especially since she had said she wasn't going to worry about her mother any more.

She really wasn't.

Her mother was just doing the same stuff over and over again. It was better to have a Christmas same as ever and her mother drinking a little and talking a lot about Daddy and not crying real quiet and not eating or sitting at the living room window all the time. Wasn't it better to talk about Daddy? Talking didn't hurt people —except when she was talking to Mr. Willie Williams and Miss Geneva sometimes. Her mother had even said, "I might come on over to that Kwanza mess—you and me and Marvin!"

She had even bought her mother's Christmas and Kwanza gift—had gone all the way to an African store in Harlem, that morning, to get it—a long African dress, with the back out. And she had bought all the gifts her mother would give there too. A wooden cross for Mr. Willie Williams and cloth the lady said was bright green and pretty for a gele for Miss Geneva. And some stationery with a Black man's fist on it for Mr. Dale. The paper felt nice and heavy and she hoped the drawing was okay. And then she had asked for some stationery for a real old man and the lady had said, "Well, if he's Black, maybe the note card with a pen and ink sketch of a Black family might do." And Muffin had bought the small, square package. She'd knock on Mr. Thomas's door on one of the seven Kwanza days and just give it to him, from her and Momma.

In fact, everything was working out perfectly. Except for Ernie.

Ernie didn't have any problems and that's why he couldn't understand things. His father hadn't been murdered: he was a long-distance truck driver and when he came home he was real nice. And his mother and the other six kids, Ernie's sisters, had a lot of fun. With Ernie out of the house all day—either in school or out of school now and working all day in the market—Muffin was sure they just laughed and played all the time. Ernie was the oldest and the only boy and the meanest. He probably never talks to them, Muffin thought. Just like now, with me.

"Well, why can't you tell me if you like this pattern?" Muffin asked, trying to get him to answer. Why couldn't he understand that saying she wasn't going to worry about her mother any more didn't mean she *really* wasn't going to worry. It just meant she was going to think only about the good things that happened. "You can at least tell me what kind of style would look nice or something. I mean *I* can't see styles!" Maybe that would do it. Make him answer. "I mean you're the one taking me and everything—I guess. Even though I'll just have to stand around and find somebody to talk to since you just keep stamping prices on a bunch of dumb cans and won't talk to nobody when you see they're just standing up here trying to ask you a plain dumb old question!"

Ernie was just trying to make her feel guilty—just because she felt happy.

It wasn't *his* mother, it was her mother and she knew what she was doing. She always had to know what she was doing.

Muffin could hear Ernie still punching the metal marker down on the tops of cans and stacking the cans on a shelf. She took her cane and moved it about and found his hands and poked at them a little. "If I had my Black Cinque, I'd sic him on you!"

Ernie said nothing and Muffin felt silly using the cane to touch him and she drew it back. "Ernie, will you please tell me why you're acting so funny!"

Muffin could hear the gears of the stamper click in the quiet.

"I mean I don't know what kind of lawyer you're going to be," Muffin teased. "When people come to ask for advice you'll just be looking at them or else you're just going to keep right on doing what you're doing and won't be paying them no mind!" But the teasing didn't help Muffin because she knew, knew why Ernie was angry with her. But he was wrong. Her mother would be all right. Caring about Kwanza didn't mean she didn't care about her mother. It was just that she didn't know how to say things the right way, the way she really meant them. Why couldn't he understand that? She could understand how he liked to be quiet, the *regular* quiet Ernie—not the quiet, *mad* one.

She heard Ernie get up and throw an empty carton atop other boxes in the back. And she could hear the pile shift. She heard him break open another carton and come back in the front store and begin to stamp prices again. She waited for him to say something.

But Ernie got up twice to wait on customers and sat down again and continued pushing the metal plunger against the metal cans.

"People won't even know if you're on their side or not!" He could say *something*, Muffin said to herself. Maybe she should leave, but she didn't want to leave.

"I'm on your side when you're right," Ernie said. "But you're not right now. You're letting Kwanza and what you want get in the way of seeing what's really happening—it's like riding a horse backward. He can be a great horse but if you ride him that way, you can't see where you're going. It's wrong." Ernie stopped stamping cans and Muffin knew he was looking at her, knew it, could feel it.

"Ride a horse backward—that's dumb, Ernie. Nobody does that!"

She knew he was still staring at her.

"Right! I know you're staring, I know you know how to stare at people. But my mother and Kwanza have nothing to do with horses and I don't know why you can't even understand that! So you can just keep right on staring. That's how you're going to win all your cases —by staring at people! The judge and the jury and everybody's just going to say 'Let him win, please, so we can all go home and get away from all his staring!' But staring doesn't bother me that much—people stare at me all the time. I just close my mind to it unless they're staring because of something Momma is doing."

Muffin yanked her packages up from the counter and pushed the pattern back into its bag and moved her glasses closer to her eyes and put her hand on her cane just so. "Well," she said, feeling suddenly depressed. "It's time for me to go home and cook dinner and get started on my dress—I've only got four days, including today, left before Kwanza. Mr. Dale's supposed to cut it out for me today. So, even if you don't like the style, I guess I do. It's just a dress."

"Don't go," Ernie said and started stamping cans again.

And Muffin didn't want to go and so she leaned sideways against the counter and propped her head up with her hand, elbow on the Formica. "Ernie," she said quietly. "I have a feeling everything's going to be all right. I really mean it. It's working out. Momma had the right idea to make this Christmas the kind Daddy would want us to have and the more I think about it, the more I like it. All she's doing is drinking but not a *real* lot and I mean she's not drinking more than anybody in the whole world and plus, she doesn't beg for her medicine any more. And when she drinks a little, she sleeps better and sleeps all night long. And the only place she goes— I mean *most* of the time—is over Mr. Dale's bar and everybody over there knows her and knew my father too. So I know nobody's going to bother her. All they do is fuss a lot. And the only other place she goes when she's sad is sit over at the cab company."

"You're saying the exact opposite of what you said last week!" Ernie said.

"But things have changed! I even managed to get Momma to put on her good coat Daddy bought for her, the heavy one—instead of that thin old jacket of his she wears, when we went to get the record player. It worked when I said that if she wore her good one, it'll be like Daddy was there keeping her warm. At first, she just said, 'Shut up, Marvina, you talk too much!' but then she put it on." Muffin stopped and thought for a second. "In a way, I'm real surprised how she's changed," she said. "Maybe the whisky even helps her a little. The only thing she does is talk a lot and go to sleep."

"Drinking whisky won't help," Ernie said, "and it looks like she's getting more unreal and I think you better check yourself."

"Check myself! Check me!" This time she was angry. Really angry. He hadn't even listened to all she had said. "You're the one," she said loudly. "You're the one acting funny, Ernie. You and Momma—not me! And it's not even Momma, it's you! Yesterday you said don't crowd her and stick with her and now that everything's better —you're acting funny! I mean you're acting like everything I say and everything I do is wrong, ever since I said I'm not going to worry any more, since I said yes, I'm *going* to Kwanza. But you never say anything when I do stuff you think is right! Nobody does! And it's just me and my mother and me figuring out what to do. Well, I've figured out what to do one more time and it's to let Momma have the kind of Christmas she wants and when Christmas is over, she'll stop drinking and trying to say things to hurt people and everybody understands but you!"

Muffin grabbed her packages tight again and some were slipping and she pulled them up and moved her cane away from the tangled bunch of bags and didn't look toward Ernie and opened the door. This time she was really going. "So, anyway, Ernie," she hollered back though she didn't need to in the small store. "You're right! I *am* going to check myself out and I'm going to check myself into the prettiest and the yellowest and the most velvet dress to the floor I can make! And you don't have to take me to the festival either. I think I cut and sprinkled enough sparkles on those black construction paper mobiles to just be able to go! By myself! Just go! Or maybe Mr. Dale will go with me and he'll take me to another one of those fabulous restaurants—the Black ones—like that pretty-feeling place in Harlem. Maybe I couldn't see it, but it was pretty and I *knew* it was pretty and everybody there knew it was pretty. Especially, Mr. Dale!

"I'll even dance by myself at Kwanza! I'll just float under those lights you put up to go with *my* mobiles and I'm going to say to myself, 'Muffin, you're okay.' And I'll just float, just dance! In fact, when the celebration is over that night—I'll just sit down and wait for the other six nights and days of Kwanza—and I'll start dancing all over again and I won't even stop when the Karamu begins. I'll still be dancing under those black sparkling mobiles, just me and my yellow dress!"

"No matter what?"

"No matter what, Ernie! I'm going to the Black Museum's Kwanza Festival even if I stop breathing. I'm going even if the world ends! I'm going—I mean—I'm going no matter what! I'm going! And I know what's bothering you—it's that you can't feel sorry for me. That's all you do sometimes is feel sorry for me! Well, now that Momma's happy, I'm happy too!"

"Your mother's not happy," Ernie said.

"You're going to tell me what *my* mother is!"

"She's not gaining ground, she's losing it. She's talking unreal—and it's real to her. I've noticed that and I think you should notice that. Instead of getting her to Kwanza, maybe we can get her back to the clinic again. You're missing the whole point of Kwanza. It's not a dress. It's knowing."

Muffin slammed the door so hard the rim shook.

But walking down the street toward her house, Muffin 89

began to feel good again and she really wasn't angry with Ernie. I wish I could shout Happy Kwanza to everybody, she thought, and let them see me—everybody—in my Kwanza dress, my lemon yellow panne velvet Kwanza dress!

Muffin glided up the carpeted steps. Tank was in the hall; and she didn't care about the bad smell of him and she didn't care about the upstairs sound of Mr. Thomas opening his door. And Muffin almost yelled out she had a present for him. She would get something for Tank too. She'd forgotten about him.

It didn't even matter about Mr. Thomas peeping out; let him peek. The *main* thing about today was that Mr. Dale was cutting out her dress.

The Kwanza dress!

All she had to do now was to take the pattern up to him. Then pray to God he liked it.

But Muffin felt good, felt like singing, felt as if she were bursting with some kind of magnificent-feeling Black thing. What Ernie said hadn't hurt her. It was just that he didn't understand. She knew what Kwanza meant because, right then, suddenly, it was like Kwanza had already come for her.

But when she opened the door to her apartment, Muffin stopped short, walked in and slipped on something. A pungently sour, acrid smell smashed into her.

Vomit.

TEN

MUFFIN WALKED GINGERLY into her mother's bedroom and held tight to her cane and her packages, frightened, to where the smell and the mess she was stepping in was worst and found her mother lying across the bed sleeping. Muffin felt around, not with her cane but with her hand, and discovered the lumpy, runny slime was all over her mother and all over the bed. And on the floor—a pillow in it.

There was also the unmistakable odor of urine and Muffin knew further how sick her mother had been.

She listened now to the labored breathing and it didn't sound any different from the last time she had drunk too much and vomited.

Muffin, her packages and cane bunched up in one arm now, felt over her mother again and touched the picture she held tightly to her thin chest. Except for one corner of the velour-backed frame, it had been protected from the foul flow.

Muffin ran down the hall to her room, slipping again, and threw her packages on the bed and didn't hook the cane over the wooden pineapple but threw her glasses on the dresser and opened her closet and felt all over the bottom of the plastic bag with the lemon yellow velvet.

The medicine felt the same. Her mother hadn't touched it.

Thank God.

Muffin went into the bathroom and put her cane in the tub and washed it and rinsed it and wiped it off and took it back in her bedroom and hooked it over the wooden pineapple. No need to remove her shoes. She would have to wash all the floors except the kitchen—and even maybe the kitchen. She hadn't gone in there yet. She did then. Her mother had gotten sick there too, on much of the sink. Muffin went back to her bedroom and sat down on her bed and faced the darkness and tried to think and couldn't think and got up and discovered she still had on her pea jacket and felt it and it was clean and she hung it up in her closet.

She sat back down on the bed and started crying and couldn't stop the quiet tears.

Nothing works out, she said softly to herself. Nothing works out. Maybe Ernie's right and maybe Momma's getting worse and if she gets worse and worse—what's going to happen?

Muffin lay back on the bed and remembered that her mother had vomited just as badly several weeks ago and she had been all right. This was no different. Why was she alarmed? Why was she crying like a baby? Crying was just a waste of time.

It was Ernie's fault. He was making her afraid with his dumb remarks. Everything was all right and there were things to do. Muffin got up from the bed. The very first thing was to get some air into the house. But when Muffin went back into her mother's room she decided it was too cold outside to fully open the window in there and let the wind blow in on her mother and maybe make her get pneumonia or something.

She opened all the living room windows wide and closed her mother's door a bit.

The second thing she had to do was clean her mother up. But Muffin washed her own face first and tried to feel better.

Vomit was vomit. It wasn't blood.

Muffin sat down on the tip edge of her mother's bed for a few moments and felt her mother's shoes and took them off her and told herself she would go ahead with her plans for what was left of the day. When she had finished cleaning up her mother, she would go upstairs to Mr. Dale's and stay there while he cut out the Kwanza dress. Then she'd come back and open up a can of soup for dinner—and one for her mother later if she wanted to eat, if she could eat. Otherwise she wouldn't wake her mother up, wouldn't disturb her, would let her sleep, while she, Muffin—sewed.

Then, while Muffin was walking down the hallway to the bathroom, trying to close down her brain against the smell, she decided not to clean either her mother now, or the room, but go up to Mr. Dale's first.

Maybe it would help to run away for a while.

Muffin went quickly back to her room and got the pattern and yanked open the closet again and grabbed the plastic bag down and emptied it of all the plastic and glass vials and hid them under her mattress and then threw the bag over her arm. Then she double-bolted her door and practically flew up the steps to Mr. Dale's.

Muffin knew it wasn't Mr. Dale who opened the door. She tried to keep her voice from breaking. "Is Mr. Dale here?" she managed to ask.

"Hey, Dale!" the man called back. "Little girl to see you, man."

"Muffin, my lifesong! Come in! Talk to me!"

Muffin walked in, but she hated it when Mr. Dale had company. "I just wanted you to help me cut the pattern out," she said. "I wanted to sew it tonight." Muffin, listening very hard, was trying to read the man standing behind her. She hated him. "But you have company."

"No matter, Black love, you shall have your dress cut! Clarence," Mr. Dale was saying, "meet the sweet precious balance in my life—Miss Muffin Johnson!"

"Hi," Muffin managed, hating the man.

"Leave the pattern," Mr. Dale said. "I'll cut it and drop it off on my way out. How's Leola? I heard she was across the street this morning."

"Fine," Muffin said and walked back toward the door, the lovely shag carpet feeling spongy—ushy under her feet. She really did hate it when Mr. Dale had company.

Mr. Thomas was opening his door and Clarence was whispering, "The kid blind?"

I hate you!

"Hell, no!"

When Muffin got back downstairs and opened her door, the smell seemed worse. The open windows hadn't made any difference. The pattern and the panne velvet and Mr. Dale and an intruder named Clarence faded from her mind. It was time to help her mother.

I shouldn't even have gone up to Mr. Dale's, she told herself. But now I'm back and that's just that.

Muffin went into the bathroom and reached under the tub and thought for a moment about the dog she'd have eventually. "I'm glad, Black Cinque," she said aloud, "you're not here. You'd just be running around and making a worse mess." But Muffin wished a little that he was there already. She felt like talking and it was dumb to talk out loud to yourself.

She pulled the basin from under the tub and filled it with water and pine disinfectant and went back to her mother's room and began to wipe away the recoiling textured liquid.

But it seemed to Muffin that she was getting nowhere and she was beginning to feel too sick inside and she wanted to cry and she wasn't sure exactly why.

By the time Muffin had wiped most of the ropy mass away from her mother on the bed and had eased the framed photograph Leola was holding so tightly away from the folded arms, she wasn't crying and she was angry. And it didn't make her feel any better when she recognized the framed portrait.

It was her baby picture.

I just don't care, Muffin said inside over and over and finally tiptoed out of the room and threw the sour spew from her mother down the toilet and rinsed out the basin and flushed the toilet and didn't know why she was crying again. She poured some pine in the toilet and swished the sticky cloth around and around in it   95 and flushed the toilet again and cried harder and rinsed the cloth out again.

"Oh, no!" Muffin yelled out loud, her tears suddenly stopping—suspended there in the darkness. *My long slip!* Muffin flipped open her watch and read the dial. "I've got an hour and a half," she said. "The saleslady leaves at six!" Muffin panicked. *She'll think I'm crazy!*

Muffin washed her hands quickly. *She'll think I'm nuts! Plus she said she wouldn't be back in the store until after Christmas!* Muffin opened the bathroom cabinet and took out her father's pic and practically raked it through her hair. *She even bought it on her own lunch break so she'd have time to find me a nice one!* "She'll think I'm terrible if I don't get over there and get it and give her her money back!"

Muffin threw on her pea jacket and opened her wallet to see how much money she had—so much had happened today that she couldn't remember things.

One ten-dollar bill, folded the long way. A five-dollar bill folded the short way and three one-dollar bills folded in quarters. And a dollar and sixty-five cents in coins.

She'd take a cab and get back quick.

Muffin had unhooked her cane from the wooden pineapple when the doorbell rang two short rings.

Ernie!

"Good," Muffin said, closing her mother's door and hoping Ernie couldn't smell the vomit, which was silly since the whole house smelled like it. "He can drive me and I can get back real fast."

ELEVEN

"ERNIE, LEAVE HER ALONE!" Muffin wanted to yell, to scream, to make the fullest and loudest noise she was capable of, but she couldn't. She could only whisper again, "Don't wake her *up*, Ernie!"

Muffin pulled back on Ernie's shoulders, tried to push his hands away from her mother and couldn't. She put her hands on her mother's face and felt him washing the crusty and partly dried deposits there with the washcloth and towel he had yanked out of the linen closet. He was using two basins—one for the first washing and the other, with a piece of old perfumed guest soap and fresh water, for the second washing.

Leola, except for an occasional grunt, did not wake up.

Once she had murmured something Muffin couldn't understand and she didn't care, didn't want to understand. Muffin was keyed to the movements of Ernie and not to the sounds of her mother.

"Get something clean on her," Ernie said. "I'll fix up the room and the bed."

"You don't have to come in here and make beds or fix rooms, Ernie! Please leave—I mean, I can do it. I'm just not *ready* for Momma to wake up yet. I just *told* you I have to go get my long slip before six o'clock or the saleslady's going to think I'm crazy to say *nothing* about owing her money! I was going to finish washing up everything as soon as I got back!"

Ernie went into the bathroom and Muffin could hear him pouring the used water from both basins down the toilet and flushing it. She heard him rinse them out and fill them up again and place them in the bathtub. Then she heard him get the old scrub pail from beneath the sink and fill it with water and pour in the pine disinfectant. She listened to him put the scrub pail in the hall and take the two basins out of the tub. "Wash her and change her clothes in the living room," he said, walking past Muffin and down the hall, through her mother's bedroom and into the living room. Muffin followed and heard the clink of the basins when he placed them on the glass part of the coffee table. She heard him go back for the scrub pail and put it on her mother's floor. "I'll put her on the sofa," he said. And Muffin heard him open the linen closet again and take out something and come back in the living room and spread it on the sofa.

It was a sheet.

"Who told you to come up here, Ernie? You just tell me who told you to come up here!"

"Mr. Williams."

"Mr. Willie Williams?"

98   Muffin heard Ernie pick her mother up off the bed

and come in the living room and place her gently on the sofa.

Leola woke up. "Don't push me, Marvina," she demanded hoarsely, thick-tongued. "You leave me be—leave—"

"It's not me bothering you, Momma, I'm not doing it, Momma—you go back to sleep." But before Muffin could finish speaking her mother was already snoring again.

"I said fix her up."

"No! I told you I had to run out for a minute and you're just doing this to make me feel bad like you tried to do in the store today. I've washed up the floor and the bed already—and I was coming back to do all this, Ernie! And I was stupid enough to be glad when you rang the bell because you could take me and get me back fast because you know how hard it is for me to get a cab to stop for me sometime—"

"Her clothes stink—I've washed her face and neck and arms but that puke's all over her. The bed stinks and the room stinks. How can you want her to sleep like that?"

Ernie's voice was too quiet. She had explained to him and he had no reason to be angry. "I *told* you I was only going to pick up the long slip—" Why was she whispering?

"Just like that?"

"Yeah, Ernie! Just like that!" This was the worst day of her life. He was really angry and it didn't make sense to her. Why was he making it such a big thing? "Momma was sick just like this a few weeks ago and

I did it—cleaned her up and washed everything—by myself!" Ernie always understood things. How come he couldn't understand now? Wasn't she coming right back? And if Ernie could drive her, couldn't she get back even faster?

Ernie was pulling open dresser drawers.

"Ernie," Muffin whispered again and didn't know why again. Her mother was snoring. "What are you doing?"

"Looking for a nightgown."

"No! I told you I'm not going to disturb Momma—"

"That's okay," Ernie said. "I'll do it."

"Change my mother!"

"Change your mother."

Muffin stood there and couldn't believe it but did believe it. "You're crazy," she finally whispered. "You're crazy, Ernie. You're nuts! You got more nerve than—"

But even while Muffin fussed she started to remove her mother's clothes quickly. She didn't dare touch her watch. And though she got up and slammed shut the door between her mother's bedroom where Ernie was and the living room where she was, she felt glad suddenly that Ernie was there, glad he was helping her.

He was pulling and wrapping into a bundle the bed linens when she walked back into the room. "Crazy people," she muttered close to him and pulled a nightgown out of a drawer.

But Ernie came over and took another gown from the open drawer. When Muffin felt the lace collar on it, she put it back. "Momma'll have fits if she wakes up and finds herself in that! Daddy gave it to her last Christmas."

"Put something pretty on her."

"I'm not talking to you," Muffin announced and walked back into the living room, straightening out with her feet a small scatter rug crumpled near the sofa. "All my mother's clothes are pretty! Nobody told you to come up here getting in the way. The whole thing is Momma's not a real whisky drinker and when she drinks too much she gets sick. If Mr. Dale had been over there, this wouldn't have happened."

"He's never in the bar in the daytime."

Muffin couldn't answer then. She had thought the same thing when she had come in and found her mother. Why had she gone to the Midnight Club so early in the day?

But Muffin pushed the question quickly back again. Saturday was Christmas and after that it would be over. All her mother had to do was make it through that one day. Then it would be Kwanza and not Christmas.

Kwanza. When she would wear her beautiful dress. *And with a slip under it I hope!*

Muffin, washing her mother's back, realized suddenly that her mother had stopped snoring, that her breath seemed to be caught too long. She bent over her mother and had a fright.

She couldn't hear any breathing at all!

But then, in a burst, the loud snoring came again and Muffin felt a quick but solid disgust. She also felt sadness. And part of the sadness was for herself.   101

Muffin leaned back against her mother's legs and listened to Ernie washing the bedroom floor, sloshing the pine-scented water back and forth with a mop. In her mind, Muffin could see the water soaking into the familiar worn spots on the linoleum. She felt her mother's hand hit her thigh and fall limply against the sofa edge. "Marvina, what you do—?" her mother mumbled. "I'm asleep! Move off my legs."

Muffin got up and pulled a small stool close to the couch, by her mother's head, and sat down beside the renewed snores.

She put her fingers in her mother's hair and smoothed the wispy strands back and forth, listening to her breathe. She had always liked brushing her mother's hair. Sometimes when the three of them were together in the living room, she'd sit on the sofa with her mother on the floor in front of her—leaning back—and she'd brush for hours and listen to her father talk and her mother laughing and teasing him. She would talk too, but mostly she liked to listen to them, to enjoy them. Since last Christmas, she had brushed her mother's hair even more, but Leola had been depressed, her head against Muffin's knee, crying. No laughing now. But brushing and combing her mother's hair helped Muffin to think, to plan.

Muffin was still sitting on the stool when Ernie said he was coming through and did and lifted her mother from the sofa and put her in the freshly made bed, the scent of pine disinfectant mingling with the smell of pine from the tall, scrawny Christmas tree.

"Get out my bed, boy," Leola fussed thickly, and

moved her head heavily on the crisp pillow. "Who you think you are—in my bed—"

"I'm gone," Ernie said. "You sleep."

"Marvina!" Leola managed to fuss before she turned and went back to sleep, grunting.

Muffin was halfway down the hall leading to the kitchen, realizing that Ernie had washed all the floors, when she found Ernie wasn't walking behind her. He was opening the front door. "See you later," he said and stepped into the hall.

"Ernie, wait! I need a lift—I told you I had to get to the Black department store and get my long slip for Kwanza!" Muffin flipped open her watch. *Five thirty!* "I need a lift, Ernie! I could have been there and back if you hadn't come butting in here!"

"No."

"No!"

"I'm supposed to be making a delivery. I have to go do it."

"Ernie, you know you can take me—it's not that far away. You're just acting funny, and I don't appreciate Mr. Willie Williams sending you up here!" No. She didn't mean that. She didn't mean that at all.

"He thought you might be having a hard time with her. It seems like she made it pretty rough for him earlier today and wouldn't let him bring her home and she was sick. So he came up a little while after she went in the house and saw the door was locked up all right and then called to her until she answered. Then he went away and he came back and he said he could hear her snoring. So when he told me a little while ago, I got around here as soon as I could. He wanted to come but he thought it might make things worse. But you don't have problems any more, Muffin. It's that horse I told you about. You riding him backwards and not looking where you're going, not seeing what's happening."

"See! What can I see, Ernie? Can I see you right now?" The bitterness in her own voice surprised her.

Ernie turned and walked toward the steps.

"Wait, Ernie!" Muffin cried after him. Something was coming inside her and she wanted to push it back before it choked her, overflowed and choked her. "Listen, Ernie— Listen—" Where were the words she wanted to say and they were there and jumbled up, coming too fast, disappearing too fast too.

"Listen to me, Ernie! Listen like I listen— You know—you know that big Braille Bible Mr. Willie Williams gave me, well, there's a place in it where God says behold the fig tree and when you see the leaves come you know summer is coming and—Well, I can't see things and I can't listen for a fig tree. Nobody can listen for a fig tree. And I don't care about summer any more. Summer won't ever be the same again and Christmas won't ever be the same and nothing is like it used to be."

"You riding wrong," Ernie said, going down the steps.

Muffin felt like yelling, really yelling about this long, long year when she would gladly have put herself on a horse or a train or on anything and run and never looked back. Ride backward or any way at all, to get away from the up and down days, never knowing what a day was going to be. *Asalaam alaikum* was not part of her life, not for real and not for long.

Maybe Kwanza wasn't either. Kwanza meaning first fruits, first of the harvest to come. She, Muffin knew a lot now about first things. Too many firsts had happened since her father had died on a cold, snow-banked Brooklyn sidewalk, lead-piped to death. It had been a first for her. Her mother's piercing screams in her ears had been a first too.

Four nights from now, the first Kwanza candle in her life would be lit and that would also be another first.

It was a first she was looking forward to. A first she could enjoy and she was going to enjoy it no matter what.

"Don't you worry about me," Muffin said, leaning over the rickety banister and yelling down to the first floor where she could hear Ernie. "And don't you worry about the horse I ride. He's the prettiest thing you ever saw. Sleek and black as he can be. He streaks through the wind and he doesn't need direction and I'm going where he's going. I'm riding him all the way to Africa! You helped teach me all the stuff I know about Africa — Well, Africa's mine now! I own it! So just don't worry about me!"

"Okay," the boy hollered up. And Muffin heard the broken-hinged downstairs door slam hard, and she turned around and went back into the apartment, left the door open, threw on her coat, snatched her cane from the bed post and took her glasses from the dresser and put them on, grabbed her shoulder bag, locked the apartment door and ran down the steps. She could hear Mr. Thomas quietly closing his door upstairs.

Why couldn't Ernie understand? He was the only one spoiling things for her.

Tank! "Oh, Tank—Tank, can you help get a cab for me? I think I'm going to die if I can't get one!"

"Baby, Miss Cupcake, cabs don't do no stopping for me. Sugar."

"Maybe they'll stop for the two of us together. Please help me, Tank, I'm in a hurry!"

"You got me. Come on."

A cab stopped but Tank held everything up trying to memorize the driver's number. "In case you don't make it where you supposed to be making it!" he said. Then Tank opened and closed the door several times, "Ain't no good, won't lock. Trick cab."

Not only had the saleslady bought Muffin the softest nylon slip she had ever felt in her whole life, she also handed her a brand new bottle of very light yellow dye. "Keep it plain white or dye it yellow—either way—you got a pretty slip."

In the cab on the way home, Muffin decided she wanted a yellow slip. She would ask Miss Geneva to dye it for her. She also decided she shouldn't have yelled at Ernie. Things wouldn't seem so terrible if he could just understand how she felt. *Why can't he see that I'm doing the best I can?"*

But Muffin forgot about Ernie when Miss Geneva handed her the yellow panne velvet, cut and pinned just so. "Dale brought it down and give it to me to give you when he didn't get no answer when he knocked," Miss Geneva said and patted Muffin on the back. "How come you didn't come get me, baby?" she asked. "Miss Geneva be glad to go shop with you, you know that. Don't you know that, honey?"

"Uh-huh," Muffin said and felt again for the dart markings. There were none. But the saleslady had traced darts on her. "Oh, no," she murmured out loud. "He forgot to mark the darts for me!"

"I don't know, honey. Dale left you this note, baby, done up in Braille the way you showed him."

Muffin ran her fingers rapidly along the pressed out dots. What he wrote to her was that the dress was fantastic and darts would ruin it. "Jesus"—he had written —"great!"

"How Leola doing, baby?" Miss Geneva was asking. "She come down here early this morning, said she was going over Dale's. Said you was downtown, baby. Ain't no reason why bars got to open eight o'clock in the morning!"

"Yes, ma'am," Muffin answered, practically sailing out the door. Her cane, uselessly clutched with her package, was insignificant compared to the precious velvet. "Oh," she said, turning back, package and cane slipping a bit, but not the velvet. "Thanks for doing my slip —don't dye it real dark, and you don't have to tell Momma you're doing it for me. Okay?"

"Okay, honey. Miss Geneva understands, baby."

Muffin hardly heard. She was already out the door and halfway up the steps. The Kwanza dress was cut.

Two long fronts. Two long backs. And the facings. Silk facings Mr. Dale had described in the note as "a perfect shade of matching yellow."

Her mother was not in the bed, not in the house.

I'm just going to start sewing right now, Muffin told herself, and I'll do as much as I can while Momma's out and I can concentrate. And out loud, she said, "Because if something goes wrong with this dress, I'll die. I swear I'll die."

But what went wrong that night, at exactly eleven fifty-eight according to the raised dots of Muffin's watch —dots she kept her fingers on and held on to, had nothing to do with the lemon yellow panne velvet. The slick-finish dress, partly basted, was coming along fine.

What was it her mother had just said, had just walked in the house and said?

"We can't have no kind of Christmas, Marvina. He dead. Marvin dead. We can't make out like he living. Marvin dead."

TWELVE

"How come you're not doing the stuff you said!"

"What stuff, what I say?"

"The plans you made—all the things you said."

"I ain't got no plans, Marvina. Marvin dead."

"The record player and the Duke Ellington stuff and decorating the tree and hanging fruit cake wrapped up on it and Mr. Willie Williams eating dinner with us, like he always does on the holidays—how can you just change things all of a sudden!"

"You didn't even want the record player, Marvina, you said it cost. Now, it's all right. Well, if you want it, you got it." Muffin felt her mother's bony arms swish through the air with more a halfhearted attempt to brush something away than with a deliberate, hostile motion. "I tried to talk to Willie. Willie and me used to talk about anything. I don't want no Christmas coming near this house, Marvina. I don't want it, baby! I don't! I don't!" she cried. "I don't want it, baby!"

"We should remember Daddy like you said." *I am going to my Kwanza. I am going, I am going.*

"Marvin dead!"

"We're going to do what you said," Muffin said, trying to sound matter of fact as she could. "We'll have the same Christmas you said we'd have. We'll call Grandma Johnson in Nashville, after dinner, like we always do."

"We not calling nobody. Marvin dead," Leola said and walked close to Muffin and touched her and tried to draw her close but Muffin sat stiffly at the machine and did not bend. "We should never left Nashville, you and me and Marvin. If we didn't leave to come up here —Marvin still be alive."

Muffin felt her mother's hands fall away from her, listened to her leave the room and go in the bathroom and open the cabinet. Listened to her shut the cabinet door, leave the bathroom, go into her bedroom, open the top drawer. Listened to her come back and stand close. "I need my sleeping pills. I got to sleep."

Muffin's unseeing eyes focused on her mother standing there.

"Marvina?"

Muffin got up from the stool and went to her bed and reached between her cotton ticking mattress and the box spring and pulled out the glass and plastic bottles.

"Why you got it under there?"

"You drink too much whisky," Muffin said, coldly as she could.

It didn't matter that she could feel her mother crumble a little. Muffin held one end of the heavy mattress up and reached in deeper for the rest of the vials. "You can have all your medicine, Momma. You keep it and I'm not going to worry any more about what you do and where you go and how late you go out. Period. I'm not. I loved Daddy too and Christmas will be hard. But there are happy things to do and I want to do them, be a part of them—"

"Marvina?"

"I'm going to my Kwanza—it's yours too, but you won't come. But I'm going to be there when Etta Moten Barnett comes and starts that way she has of talking. You know her words just glide in so pretty and she's a star to me and I'm going to hear her when she lifts her hands with the sound of those bracelets people say are ivory. I'm going to be there when she says that thing about Kwanza."

The medicine bottles Muffin was pouring into her mother's hands were spilling all over the floor. Muffin reached down and got them. Her mother didn't move. "This is to go to sleep and this one is to calm you down and this one makes you stop crying but you can't take it after four o'clock or else you can't sleep at all. It makes you happy but you don't sleep so good. This one with the cross scratched on top is too old and you said it didn't work—so you can just throw it away. Wait, I'll throw it away!" Muffin plopped the small tubelike bottle into her trashcan. It hit the metal with a plang!

Muffin fell back on her bed and lay there. Her words sounded broken, tears were running into her mouth. "I want to be happy," she managed to say. "I'm tired of things going wrong!"

Muffin heard her mother hesitate for a moment and

then walk slowly out of the room and for a brief moment she was sorry. But didn't she have the right to be angry?

Muffin lay there on the bed a long time and listened to her mother cry. "Marvina?" Leola called. "Marvina?"

"Yes, Momma."

"I remember that boy up here today, I remember."

"He just came by," Muffin said icily.

"He see me nasty?"

"No."

"I got up and saw the sheets and stuff in the hamper and I feel low you had to clean that mess. Momma's sorry."

"I'm not thinking about it, Momma."

"You sure that boy didn't see me? I'm trying to remember."

"He didn't."

"I don't want to be no kind of embarrassment to you like that."

"You weren't."

"You sure he didn't see?"

"I'm sure."

"I'm going crazy, Marvina."

"You're not going crazy, Momma."

"You know where I went when I woke up and you weren't here and I saw that mess in the dirty clothes?"

Muffin didn't answer.

"I went over to the cab company and I just sat there and didn't see but one person knew me and Marvin. A dispatcher. But she just smiled and didn't say nothing to me, just smiled. I guess she thought I was crazy too, wondering how come I was just there sitting. But I sat there and it seem like Marvin just was going to walk through that door and see me and say like he used to say, 'Lee, why you got that baby out in this weather? Why you got that girl sitting in this place with people talking all kinds of way?' Or, he'd be shaking his head and smiling and say, 'Lee, what's it going to be like when you can't get to me every time you want to?' I guess he knew without him I just don't count, can't make it." It was a long time before her mother spoke again.

"Don't you be like me, Marvina, don't you count on a man to be everything because they can't be with you all the time and when they gone you ain't nothing at all." There was another long pause and Leola spoke again. "Funny thing too," she said. "When you was born I was looking forward more to getting out of bed to hang around his neck then I was about you doing okay—messing with you. I guess I knew you be all right. You just looked like you be all right. Mainly it was just me and that man," the sobbing voice continued. "He said, 'Lee, don't give that baby my name—don't call her Marvina, give her her own name so she know she got one all her own.' And then he started calling you Muffin and I never did. I always say Marvina."

Muffin listened to her mother, and it seemed as if her father was in the room with her and she could see his face as clear as she saw it before she turned ten years old. And for the first time in a long while she wished he was alive again. "Tell me what to do," was what she asked him most often. "How's it coming over to you?" he'd answer.

Things were perfect then.

And if she was riding a horse backward, like Ernie said, then her father would have stopped the horse and helped her sit on it the right way.

"Marvina, remember Marvin was always so quiet and it would be just you and me doing all the talking and when we stop, he'd say, 'How come you two shut up? Neither one of you saying much of nothing but keep talking anyway.' Remember?"

"Uh-huh."

Leola Johnson didn't speak again though Muffin found herself waiting. It was quiet in the dark except for the sounds of other people, other lives, in the apartment across the airway. Laughter.

When Muffin was sure her mother was sleeping, she got up from the bed and sat back down at the sewing machine and began to baste the dress again. Maybe I'll stay up the rest of the night and finish basting, she thought. Maybe I can make it—lining and everything, tomorrow.

Muffin had almost completed basting the left front to the left back, when her mother spoke and Muffin knew she had not been asleep at all. "I hope you don't never know what lonely is."

Muffin was in bed and almost asleep, two hours later, when she heard her mother's sobbing voice again. "I rather see you dead than lonely."

THIRTEEN

"I'll make beef stew and cook it slow and sew all day," Muffin said, trying to forget it was only nine o'clock in the morning and that her mother had already gone out. I'm only going to deal with important things today, she reminded herself. And the important thing is that Momma's wearing her heavy coat. And she doesn't *have* to be going over to Mr. Dale's!

Muffin opened a cupboard and took out the timers she wanted. Tomorrow's Christmas Eve, so I'll make enough for two days, she told herself. And minutes later, Muffin was dumping two packages of special stew spices into an earthen bowl half-filled with beef chunks. Then she put flour and more spices into a paper lunch bag and put in the pieces of meat and shook the bag up and down. Then she plopped each floured cube into a huge iron pot of sizzling fat. When the meat was crusty-edged, tested by Muffin's forking each piece and touching her finger to it quickly, she poured water in the pot and put the heavy lid on and turned the fire low.

She cut up carrots and potatoes and put them into a large pot of water, took icy packages of frozen peas and frozen corn from the freezer compartment and put them in the bottom of the refrigerator. Then she remembered one other spice and took it from the rack and uncorked the small jar and pulled out several hedge-leaf-shaped, stiff bay leaves with the bitter perfumy taste Muffin had discovered once when she bit into a dry one straight from the jar. She dumped two bay leaves into the pot.

Muffin went back to her room and turned on her radio and leaned down and lightly kissed the pile of carefully folded fabric. Then while she was harmonizing with the voice of Smoky Robinson and twisting around on the desk chair, she picked up the piece of yellow silk lining that she had made so many mistakes on the night before, when she had been too tired, and felt it and put it down and picked up a needle threader and threaded a small, fine needle.

While Muffin was trying to turn the thin strip to be used for a loop for the covered button she would attach to the left side seam at the waistline, her mother came back.

"Marvina!"

"Yes, Momma," Muffin answered.

"I'm sleep, Marvina! I'm sleep!"

"Okay, Momma."

"Okay—well, okay."

Muffin listened to her mother turn heavily on the bed but she continued to sew, wasn't angry at her mother's drinking. If she was going to deal only with important things from now on, the important thing was that her mother was in and safe and that the lining had turned out perfect.

She wanted to show Mr. Dale.

"Fantastic," he said when he opened his door and Muffin could tell, could hear Mr. Thomas standing close to the other side of his. "You not jiving are you!"

"You like it? It looks okay? I know it *feels* okay but does it *look* okay—I mean really good?"

"Fantastic! Come on in."

"Nope! I have to go back down and finish!"

Muffin was halfway back down the steps when he called, "I'm treating you to shoes. Christmas present."

"Ooh," Muffin squealed. "Oooooooooh!" she squealed again and was on her way back up to hug him when she heard him slam his door. "I can't take your kisses," he said, opening the door again. "You definitely can't kiss!"

"I was only going to hug you," Muffin said, laughing.

Mr. Dale waved his hand and Muffin could hear his sleeve swish eloquently through the air. He was laughing. "Your hugs ain't too tough either!" he said, sounding quite serious. "I feel sorry for that young Black Jesus—what's his name, Ernie-God or something."

"Ernie!" Muffin cried, feeling absolutely silly standing there on the steps. "He doesn't do all that kissing and stuff. He hardly even talks!" Then suddenly Muffin had an idea and ran back up the steps to his door. Mr. Dale, please change your mind and come to Kwanza and then you can really meet Ernie and talk to him even if he doesn't talk back much. Then you'll

117

be able to see how I'm standing and everything and you'll see that I won't look like a crooked whooping crane in my dress!"

It would be perfect if Mr. Dale could be there with her and maybe he could get Momma to come and everything would be great. Everybody she loved would be right there with her to see how beautiful she looked. "Then you could even make something out of the pink suede to wear."

"Jesus!"

"I mean Kwanza is special, everybody's going to be there—the whole neighborhood!"

"I'd rather die!"

Well, I don't want to die, Muffin said to herself when she was back at the sewing machine. Momma wants to die and Mr. Willie Williams is always talking about dying and Heaven and Hell and stuff and Grandma Johnson talks about dying. Daddy didn't talk about dying but he died. And I'm not going to die at all, I'm going to live forever—me and this yellow velvet dress. And if my horse keeps going backward, I'll just ride it backward forever. I won't even care as long as I'm living.

By early evening, the stew was cold and the smell of it no longer eased into Muffin's senses. She hadn't eaten all day and she was hungry and every seam of the yellow velvet dress and the yellow silk lining was finished and felt great.

But she couldn't stop yet.

118   Muffin took the ironing board out of the long cab-

inet in the kitchen and put it up and took out the small, special pressing pieces Mr. Dale had given her two years ago. And when the temperature of the steam iron was just right, Muffin pressed her lining, making the seams lie completely flat. Then she pressed the panne velvet on the wrong side and put the ironing board back in the long kitchen closet. Then she sat down to do the tedious, and for her difficult, job of attaching the yellow silk lining to the yellow velvet. And though she had to put the ironing board and iron back up again, she didn't stop until the hems were sewn and pressed. She flipped open the dome of the suede-banded Braille watch: eight fifteen.

And the most beautiful dress in the world was on a hanger. Finished.

Muffin was about to wake her mother up so she could see the dress and both of them eat dinner together when she suddenly decided to do something else. The something else was to take a bath and fix her hair pretty and put on the yellow dress—really get dressed up and go show Mr. Dale.

She would show him she could be graceful and beautiful.

Muffin went into the bathroom and ran water in the chipped edged bathtub. She was sitting there, listening to the running water and feeling the steam in her face when the bell rang two short rings.

Ernie.

Muffin was about to press the buzzer when she decided not to. I'd rather put my dress on, she said to herself, and go show Mr. Dale how I look. But moments

later, Ernie rang the bell right outside the apartment
door and Muffin stood silently to the side of the door
and prayed her mother wouldn't wake up and Ernie
wouldn't keep ringing the bell. He can just think I'm
out, she thought. I want to put on my dress and he
can't see it yet!

Finally, Muffin heard Ernie going back down the
steps. His footsteps heavier and slower than Mr. Dale's.
But not as slow as Mr. Willie Williams'.

Mr. Dale'll really be glad to see me get all dressed
up, she thought when she heard the downstairs door
close, but Ernie probably wouldn't say anything. It
would be a waste of time to do all she had to do just
so Ernie could see, Muffin thought when she turned
the tub water off and then poured in a never-opened
old bottle of perfumed bath salts. The perfume smelled
weak but Muffin didn't care. At least she had put it in.
She would tell Mr. Dale she had put perfume in the
water and she was sure he'd be glad she did.

Muffin tiptoed into her mother's room and opened
the drawer where her stockings, always black now, were.
Muffin took them into the bathroom and lay them down
on top of her scuffed black patent leather dress shoes.
Then, before she stepped in the tub, she ran back to
her room and turned the radio up and ran back quietly
to the bathroom and jumped in the tub. She would
have stayed in a long time listening to the radio, the
way she usually did, except tonight she didn't have
the time.

Mr. Dale might decide to go to the bar early.

An hour later, the tub was rinsed and clean again

120

and Muffin, without her cane, was gliding up and down the short hall, back and forth to the kitchen and back down the hall again. The yellow panne velvet flowed about her. And for the first time since Mr. Dale mentioned it, she felt like a queen—Black girl of ancient Africa and today's Africa and ancient Black America and today's Black America and any other place he had mentioned. And what was the name she had heard at the Black Museum?

Nubian.

Well, whatever Nubian meant she felt that way too. She had washed her hair and the natural had been combed as high as she could get it. And it was full and soft and delicate. She sprayed it then with Afro-Sheen and knew it looked grand, sparkling with flecks of oil.

Muffin opened her mother's jewelry box and took out a pair of large hoops she knew were real gold, her mother had been married in them, and fastened them to her ears. Her own pierced-ear earrings were too small and nothing-feeling. And tonight she was going to look perfect when she went up and knocked on Mr. Dale's door. Mr. Thomas could open his door all he liked. When he saw her this time, he'd probably fling the door wide open!

Muffin posed again and put on her dark glasses and took them off again and did it just so and then decided she wouldn't take her cane to Kwanza since she'd be with Ernie. It wasn't good enough to go with her velvet dress.

Then Muffin practiced a way of walking so that the yellow velvet would flow, cling, flow and cling just the

121

way she wanted. "Etta Moten Barnett can't do this better than me," she said and glided down the hall again and didn't feel silly at all.

A few moments later, Muffin leaned close to her mother asleep on the bed and wanted to wake her up but didn't. She knew what her mother always said. "So, you think you look cute," was it. "You always cute—you don't need no new dress to look cute to me!" Muffin kissed her mother's hair lightly. "You ought to see me," she whispered and kissed her again. Then she thought about her father and knew he would have hugged her and told her what a good job she had done sewing the dress. Then he would have asked her which part had been the hardest to do and he would have looked that place over very carefully and he would have told her what he thought. And then his famous words: *You getting good with that sewing.*

Ernie would say something too, but she couldn't think for the life of her what.

And Miss Geneva would say, "Oh, baby!" Mr. Willie Williams would just say, "Now, that's pretty, Muff."

But there was only one person in the world who could appreciate the way the sleeves puffed up high at the shoulder seam, and clung to her arms from just below the elbows on down. Only one person who could appreciate the way the neckline draped even though her chest was almost flat, and the way her long, skinny self let the yellow velvet kind of spill off.

And that was Mr. Dale who knew everything.

Muffin pulled the spread up lightly over her mother 122 and leaned down and kissed her again.

It was time to go.

Holding the dress up, Muffin was halfway up the steps toward Mr. Dale's door when she felt somebody behind her. She stopped and turned, waited. It didn't smell like Tank. Tank didn't have the sense of heaviness this man had. She was certain it was a man.

Where had he come from? Why was he so close to her?

"Little yellow riding hood," she heard him say in a whining voice. Out of place with the size of him. "Pretty momma," he said. "Sweet thing."

And moments later, for Muffin, the lemon yellow panne velvet world exploded.

FOURTEEN

SOMEONE WAS TALKING in her ear and she didn't know who it was and then it was the old dusty smell of someone she knew.

Voices didn't make sense to her. Neither did the pieces of choking velvet. *Smash it with the cane, smash the velvet!* Spit the velvet, silk-backed gag out. Get off the crooked steps rammed against her back.

The chipped, scratched-varnish rickety sound was bleeding and Muffin reached for the banister she already held in her hand and couldn't find it and held on to it anyway and missed the heavy musty-smelling leather strap that came crashing down near her head.

Strange scream sounds behind the swooshing. Strange leather that smelled too old and Muffin tried to open her mouth to yell, to shout don't yell like that, don't yell—be quiet—don't let people hear. But she couldn't talk. The velvet was gone from her mouth but her mouth, too near the prickly carpet steps, too near the plunging strap, and pressed too tight against her mother's earring, wouldn't open.

Take the earring.

CRACK!

"No!" *Whisper!* "Please don't hit Mr. Thomas. Please don't—please!" *Momma!* "Please, he—" *Shhhh!* "Please!"

SMASH.

"You want something, old man! Old man, you want this, old man?"

THUD!

"Ongh! Onnngh!"

Mr. Thomas can't talk!

THUD!

Old bones smashed on a wall. Fists killing.

Footsteps moving down the steps, away at last. Slow run. Not fast.

Mr. Thomas's face is torn!

The smell of old dusty things was holding her too tight and the blood couldn't move and was soaking into her draped yellow velvet neckline, soaking into her carefully gathered puffed sleeve and the sleeve felt terrible against her skin.

And Mr. Thomas is bleeding too fast and the blood is moving and the banister's bleeding and Mr. Thomas can't talk. That's why he's crying. *And I can't rock the blood away.* "Don't cry Mr. Thomas." *Whisper.* Move from Mr. Thomas's tight hold, belt pressed against her ear, buckle on her ear. Hurting.

"No!" *Don't touch my door!* "My mother—my mother's in there!"

"Onnnnngh!"

"No!" *Find the cane. Where's the cane?* Knock Mr. Thomas away from my door, push him! Hard! "Don't   125 wake Momma, she's sick! She can't see us! We have to go to your house—!"

Wait!

Wait.

"Jesus Christ!"

Reach for that voice, get up the steps, reach for the voice.

Reach for the voice! Hold tight. Tighter!

"Jesus Christ!"

The dusty old blood smell was gone. Finished. Hold tight to the aged, pressed, treasured flowers in a soft sweater. Tiny bits of fur sweater, absorbing pain. Lifting pain away. Warm, furry turtleneck pressed into her skull. Hold on to the peace, don't ever let go—hold tight. Tighter!

The sweater held too, would not let her go.

"Muffin."

Don't answer, if you answer he will disappear. Oh! *Move back!* Mr. Thomas's Blood Getting on Mr. Dale! Move back! Get away—

Can't!

"Muffin—Muffin, baby."

Don't answer, don't talk.

"Muffin."

Muffin felt herself trembling and she didn't want to, tried to stop and couldn't and felt the crawling rough fingers all over her again. Stubby, broken fingernails, thick rhinoceros skin knuckles. Fat, short, crooked fingers. Baby voice. Callouses, stretched across the big palms, like rock islands in a sweat sea.

126   "Thomas! Jesus Christ!"

Don't talk to Mr. Thomas. Mr. Thomas can't answer. Mr. Thomas can't talk.

"Go get a towel—get a rag, man, press it to your face. You look like a goddamn dead man! You look worse than her. Jesus *Christ!*"

Muffin heard something else but she didn't reach for it, tried to run from it but Mr. Dale wouldn't let her go, and she tried to push him away and couldn't. And the voice was getting nearer and it wasn't a voice, it was a scream and it was getting louder. Attacking her ears and her mind.

"Aiieeeeeeeeeeh!"

Muffin drew closer to Mr. Dale and tried to pull the torn yellow dress inside her but somebody was pulling her backward and it was her mother and the screaming voice would not be still. Mr. Dale's long fingers were in her hair, holding her face to his neck. But it was she who was pressing in, trying to shut out the sound.

"Dale! Dale! Get away from my child! That's my child! Marvina!"

Muffin held tighter and she was moving and she didn't want to move.

"Marvina! Oh, my God—Marvina! Dale! Dale, she all right? Look at the blood! Dale! Marvina!"

People. Get the people out of my house, if I could I'd smash the people. Black Cinque, bite the people, bite the people, bite the people all up. Put me down, Mr. Dale and then I can get the people out my house and get away from my mother! "No! That's my mother's and my father's bed, that's not my bed! I want to go in my own room!" She was screaming now. "I want my own room! Take me in my own room! Put me down, Mr. Dale, I can walk! I can walk!"

"Dale, Marvina! Dale—wait! Don't you shut this door in my face! That's my child! Dale! *Dale!*"

The bathroom.

Feel the cold, chipped edge. Find the hammer again and be a baby again and chip the tub, chip the tub again. Bam away, bam away, kill the tub. Kill the tub. Get the hammer and kill the tub again.

"Dale! Dale! Open this damn door!"

Quiet, safe darkness. Bits of fur, soft sweater. *Quiet.* Quiet here.

"Don't let my mother in."

Quiet.

"Don't go. Please, don't leave me."

FIFTEEN

"I DON'T WANT to take a bath."

"Yes, you do."

"I took a bath, I took a bath already."

"Muffin, look at me."

"No."

"Look at me."

"No."

"Okay. We'll stay in here and we won't look at each other."

"Don't leave me and don't let Momma in."

"I won't leave."

"Don't let Momma in."

"The door's locked."

"I don't want to talk to Momma."

"I won't let Leola in."

"Dale! Dale! Unlock this door—why you go in there and lock the door? That's my child!"

Mr. Dale ignored Leola's voice and held tight to Muffin. "Feel better?" he asked.

Muffin didn't answer.

"It's over," he said. "It's over, Muffin."

Muffin dug her face deeper into his neck and held tight.

"It's over."

Muffin felt him move away from her but he kept one arm about her waist as he leaned over and put the stopper in the tub and turned on the water. Muffin could hear him putting his hand under the gushing water— breaking it. He adjusted the flow, managing to keep his arm about her, and opened the cabinet over the sink. "Not a damn thing to put in the water," he said, "not even some lousy bubble bath—nothing!" He slammed the cabinet door. "I'm going upstairs for a minute," he said.

"No!"

"I've got something to make the water feel good, make you relax."

"Momma may come in," Muffin cried in panic.

"If you lock the door behind me, she can't come in."

Mr. Dale was gone and Muffin could hear her mother talking and crying and Mr. Thomas making his strange sounds. "What Marvina doing in that bathroom? She's cut, Dale. Is she cut bad, Dale? Dale!"

"No."

"Where all that blood come from—I saw the blood! Marvina cut!"

"She's not cut and she's not bleeding. Thomas is the one cut. He hitting the man with a damn belt and the man jacking him up with a knife!" Muffin could hear Mr. Dale yelling, "How come you didn't hit on my door, do something make some sense? I was on my way to the bar, the damn phone over there's been busy and

I was going over to rip the damn thing out the wall—
and I opened the door and all this—"

"Dale! Why Marvina won't let me in!"

"Too much noise! The girl don't need all this, Leola.
Look at this—the girl don't need all this!"

"Well, I ain't no *noise!*"

Muffin was leaning against the door listening to her
mother and Mr. Thomas trying to talk to each other,
when Mr. Dale knocked. She opened it and let him in.
She heard him pop a heavy cork from a bottle and pour
some powder that plopped in the water. A light smell of
crushed flowers filled the bathroom.

"Milk bath."

Muffin didn't answer.

"It's not real milk powder," he said, putting other
bottles on the glass ledge above the tub. Each one he
clinked down took its place in Muffin's mind. "Use this
stuff in order, the way I have it here. Start from the left.
The smallest bottle is the perfume that matches the milk
bath powder—this one here in the big bottle, the one
with the cork. Use it up, if you want."

What I want is I wish I was dead.

"Rub the mess in your skin gently. Don't rush! You
got a long night." Muffin heard him put his hand in
the water and swish it back and forth and then she knew
he was sitting on the edge of the tub watching her and
then he reached for her and sat her down on the tub
edge beside him. "The cops'll be disgusted about the
bath," he said.

"The police! Please, Mr. Dale, please don't call,
please don't." She was begging. "The man didn't do 131

anything— I mean— I told you he didn't. I told you in the hall. He didn't!"

"The thing has to be reported. Half of Thomas's left cheek's hanging and Geneva's already called—she's a first-class panic button."

"Dale! Open the door!"

But Mr. Dale didn't open the door, he held Muffin and Muffin fought her tears back. The smell of the water and the quiet of him and the softness of his sweater filled her and helped her. And she was trying to hold on to it.

"I say you're kind of a clumsy crooked walking standing thing but that's not true," he said. "You are lovely. You are incredibly lovely. And it has nothing to do with a yellow velvet dress," he said, "though that helps." Muffin could hear his smile. "You're just a lovely thing. Period. And there will always be men who will want you just as that monster did—but it will be different. It will come differently to you. The monster is sick—he's sick because you're a child and he knew you were a child and so he's sick. Muffin—forget. Forget. You must not be frightened too long of him or you will get sick too. Thomas didn't let him do what he tried to do—and what he tried to do has happened to women forever. It's always going to happen to them. It happens to Black women every day. But you must go on. Stay strong and go on, baby."

"He was a Black man," Muffin managed to say, squeezing words past the hard knot, the choking lump in her throat.

132   "He's a sick brother—a real sick brother and what

you have to hope for is somebody to help him. We are all sick in some ways but most of the time people can't see it. You see what you want to see. I see what I want to see in you—" he said very quietly, "and you see what you want to see in me. Forget him."

Muffin didn't want to answer, didn't know how. Wanted to say things and didn't know what to say. Better to lean on him and smell the good smell of him. But while she sat there, her long dress damp with blood, she began to tremble. Muffin felt Mr. Dale's arms tighten about her.

"You know why this happens to Black women?"

Muffin tried hard to stop shaking.

"All of you—each one, nobody left out—are so incredibly beautiful, profoundly beautiful. Leola talks too much but she's beautiful too. Magnificently and incredibly beautiful and she's filled up with so much love, overflowing with love. Ageless, incredibly perfect love. And, see—people like to touch that. Want to hold that."

Muffin was shaking worse, the tremble she felt was getting deeper.

"You need me to go," he said, "now. To say nothing of Leola. She's about to have a coronary. But promise me you'll be able to go through with the rest of the night —the police, the hospital. Take the good things out of it." He paused for a moment. "What say?"

"What're they going to do at the hospital? I don't want— I mean—I mean he didn't do anything! He just, he just started and then Mr. Thomas came and hit him a lot with the belt—but—I don't want to have a baby—"

"You won't have a baby. Is that what you're saying? You said he didn't touch you, Muffin. What happened? Tell me what happened."

"He almost."

"You won't have a baby."

Muffin held her head closer to him. "I don't want a baby, like Queenie did. Remember when Queenie had a baby and the same thing happened to Queenie and Queenie didn't tell anybody and when she had that baby, she jumped off the roof. Remember when Queenie jumped off the roof—"

Mr. Dale touched her face. "Your face is swelling fast," he said. "Get bathed so we can get you to the hospital and get fixed up. You won't have a baby. I'd feel sorry for the baby."

He was standing now, away from her.

"I feel bad and I feel sick. And I'm not coming out the bathroom. I'm not."

Mr. Dale turned off the water and sat back down on the rim of the tub with her. "There's silk in the water," he said. "Waiting for you."

Muffin didn't care about silk in the water, she wasn't coming out of the bathroom.

The crushed flowers were too silent. But she didn't care about that either.

"I want you to listen for something," Mr. Dale finally said. "Promise me you'll listen for something?"

Muffin didn't answer.

"Promise?"

"I don't know if I can listen for anything. I don't want to."

"Muffin."

"Yes?" she said after a while.

"Listen for your growing-up time. It's not far away now—and you have to watch so you don't miss it," he said softly. "It's quiet."

"I don't want to grow up."

"Okay," Mr. Dale said, getting up off the tub edge.

This time when Mr. Dale left, her mother tried to push into the bathroom. He wouldn't let her. "If you go in, you'll act like you got no sense," he said.

"I don't need to act like I got no sense, that's my child! I want to be in there with her—that's *my* child!"

Miss Geneva was crying real hard.

Muffin hung the lemon yellow panne velvet dress and the slip she had run down to get that afternoon from Miss Geneva on a hook screwed into the door and removed her mother's stockings, now twisted about her knees, and one of her shoes. She couldn't remember walking in only one and she didn't care where the other one was. She never wanted to wear them again.

And when had she taken off her glasses, clutched now in her hand?

SIXTEEN

MUFFIN WAS TAKING her fourth bath when she heard the police come into the house and one of them say she wasn't supposed to take a bath.

"She's taking this one, baby!" Mr. Dale exclaimed. "You two don't have to *see* nothing—you not doctors! Just write down what I say—cause I know for a fact you two don't have to *see!*"

"Who are you?"

"Barrington Augustus Laurence Dale. Esquire!"

"Who're you to the young lady?"

"Her fine Black brother! Write that down."

"How long's she going to be in there in the tub?"

"Long as she natural want."

But Muffin got out of the tub when she heard her mother crying, saying, "This never would happen if my husband, Marvin Louis Johnson—her father—the one you let die like a dog last Christmas while you ask questions and didn't call no kind of ambulance and when it came, it came too late and he died with a street full of cops."

"They didn't come to hear that mess, Leola," Mr. Dale was saying. "Thomas can't talk. Don't you talk— I'll talk! Don't be embarrassing that girl when she comes out here."

"Marvina my child! I ain't letting nobody embarrass my child! That's you too. You included!"

Muffin slipped out of the bathroom, the lemon yellow panne velvet wrapped about her again—wet with places of sweat and blood and a stranger—and walked silently down the hall to her room and opened the door without making a sound and went inside and closed the door and dropped the heavy, clinging, flapping dress.

It hadn't felt heavy before.

Terrible, terrible, terrible dress. Hated dress. Press it deep down in the trashcan and hide the trashcan in the closet.

Muffin took her can of baby powder from the dresser and poured it into her hand and rubbed hard all the places where she felt a bit of damp and then she tried to find her clothes and couldn't find her clothes and couldn't find anything and sat down on her bed and rubbed her fingers over the powder places and wanted to rock quietly and did and it didn't work. She got up and tried to find her clothes again.

Sweaters here, not underwear. *I can't see!* Darkness! Hate the darkness.

No. No! Feel safe in the dark. Bring the black closer, wrap in it.

Finally, Muffin was dressed and her hair was combed somehow and her glasses were on and she had her cane and her mother's earrings were on the dresser and she opened the door and walked down the hallway toward the living room.

Her mother sprang forward and hugged her so hard she couldn't breathe. But that wasn't important. She wasn't trying to breathe, she was trying to get to Mr. Dale, to be with him. Mr. Dale got up and took Muffin's hand and sat down on the sofa next to her. Leola leaned over and hugged Muffin and didn't stand up again, but kept smoothing and patting Muffin's hair and kissing her.

"For God's sake, Leola!"

"My baby," her mother was saying. "My baby."

Mr. Dale reshaped Muffin's hair with his own pic and had to keep yelling at her mother. "Leave her hair alone —just get, get your hands out her hair! Every time I— Leola!"

"Marvina my child!"

Muffin sat there and held tight to one of Mr. Dale's hands and tried not to answer the questions and wanted to be back in the bathroom alone, back in the slippery, sweet-smelling water.

The dress! "No!"

But Mr. Dale went back and Muffin heard him opening the closet door and heard the metal can scrape against the door track and she could feel it when it was there in the living room, could feel it swish in the air when the policeman nearest to her handed it to the other one.

"Marvina won't cry! Marvina, cry, baby— Cry, Marvina! You feel better if you cry. Marvina! Cry!"

138   "Jesus!"

"You're Muffin, Marvina. Marvina or Muffin? What?"

"M-A-R-V-I-N-A J-O-H-N-S-O-N," Mr. Dale spelled out. *We* call her Muffin."

"Right," her mother said. "Marvina named after her father Marvin Louis Johnson—Marvina Louisa Johnson—and if he was here right now you wouldn't be standing in my house still with your hat on! Now put that in your Black pipe and smoke it. If I'm Black and you Black—you shouldn't be standing in my house with your hat on. Ain't that right? Damn right, it's right!"

After a while, it was time to leave, to go.

Muffin felt the people, felt the crowd, as soon as they got outside. She drew back to Mr. Dale, kept her head down.

"Walk. Look strong. Everybody out here's on your side. They love you."

"Right on, Marvina!" Deeta yelled.

"Don't worry none about the people," her mother was saying too loud, holding her arm too tight. "You don't have nothing to be shame of, better not let me hear nobody say Marvina Johnson got something to be shame of."

Muffin kept her head against Mr. Dale's shoulder in the police car.

But the car didn't move and the crowd pressed closer and Muffin felt stuffed up with people.

Finally, Mr. Dale said Mr. Thomas had come out and was in the ambulance.

Kings County Hospital started the questions all over and Muffin was shaking again. She wanted to get off the narrow paper sheet. And look through the dark and see the cool clearing in the woods. Touch the lake. Let the beautiful lemon yellow velvet dress float too, swirl, move gently about in the water. Black horse at the edge. Waiting.

Grab the doctor.

"A needle. Relax."

The doctor's face is too close, push the doctor's head away. Short bush. Like Daddy.

"Good girl. Good girl."

The lake is gone and won't come back. But her father's shoulders are here and she's on them and he's running and laughing and she's laughing and then he was gone and she was running alone and the yellow dress was torn and the horse was running away from her. Feel the horse and the horse is falling. Daddy! Swollen head, eyes mashed in, can't find the eyes, don't touch his head! That's his daughter. Don't let the child touch him again. Somebody get that girl back. Daddy! It's me— Daddy! Muffin! Daddy! Earring on the carpet. Pick it up. Can't! Pull hard! Pull! Pick up the earring! Daddy— it's me—can't leave the earring.

"Leave me alone!"

"Wake up."

"No!"

"Good girl!"

Sick, help me. Dizzy. Ice cold metal basin pressing against her lips.

"Good girl."

Get the nurse's hands away. *Get the cane—*

"I'm sick—I can't sit up!" *I'm sick.*

"You're sitting up already. Good girl!"

"Sick." *I'm sick.*

"Lie back and rest if you want," the nurse whispered. "But you can't go back to sleep, honey, you've been sleeping over an hour."

"Everything's all right," the doctor said. "Your bruises will be gone long before summer. So don't throw your bikini away."

Lie back.

"Sit up," the doctor said, laughing a little. "I bet if we let her go, she'll run."

Muffin went to sleep and woke up again and the doctor was still too close. "Can we talk?" he asked.

Don't answer. Where was Mr. Dale?

"Any questions?"

"No!"

"If you think of some, will you call me—Dr. Johns—here at the hospital?"

Leave my hair alone. Mr. Dale can fix it. Leave my hair alone.

"If you have to talk to somebody, will you let me know?"

"Yes." Get your hands off my hair. "Can I go home now?" The doctor's hands are too small. Push them away.

"Yes."

Get down from the table. Sick.

"You're doing fine. This prescription is for something to make you rest—that's what you need now. You think you need something else?"

"No."

"The police will pester you for a while—though maybe not. They've mentioned the name Pitts. I understand your description and what the old gent wrote fits somebody they know about."

"I don't care."

"Right," the doctor answered. "I know that."

"I don't!"

"Right."

Don't say right again.

"May I go now?"

"Feel okay?"

"Yes."

"Good girl."

Muffin wanted to go and then she didn't and the name Pitts was trying to get out of her remembering mind and the cold room was warm now and the doctor's voice was soft and she wanted to thank him and couldn't. What would she thank him for? What did he do? What had he said? He had said she wouldn't have to jump off the roof like Queenie. But Queenie did, she had told him. Queenie did. Queenie jumped. Queenie died.

It was easy when you died.

Muffin, back in the emergency waiting room, the doctor's arm about her, heard Mr. Willie Williams' voice. But that wasn't what she felt suddenly. It was somebody else. A wet summer forest in the rain.

Ernie!

"I've got the car," Ernie said. "When everybody's ready, we can go."

SEVENTEEN

"Stop bugging Muffin," Mr. Dale was saying, pushing Leola's hand away from Muffin's face. "Or ride in front with Jesus!"

"Jesus don't know you!" Leola cried.

Muffin listened to her mother and Mr. Dale on either side of her and felt like laughing for the first time in a million years. Ernie didn't know Mr. Dale was talking about him and not God.

"This your car, Dale? You can't tell me where to sit. This is *my* child here, it ain't your child. You think it's your child but it ain't! That one up there driving mine too. Can you drive? You know you can't! You can't drive and this ain't your car!"

"I don't need to drive, Leola! I got people drive me anywhere I want! I can find more people to drive me than you can find to drive you. Come on. Deal with that."

"I can deal with you all right but Willie in this car and my child in this car and that child driving in this car and you and me can't talk right now."

"Talk your talk. But *don't* bug Muffin tonight!"

Muffin kept her head on Mr. Dale's shoulder and wished Ernie would say something. What was he thinking about?

"I guess we should stop, Leola, before we get back," Mr. Willie Williams said. "You—maybe Muff needs something."

"You want something, sugar?" her mother asked and kissed her twice. "You want a soda or something or some ice cream? What you want?"

"Johnny Walker Black," Mr. Dale said.

"Dale! You don't respect nobody. My child don't drink no whisky!"

"I didn't say nothing about whisky. I said Johnny Walker Black."

"Pull over," Mr. Willie Wiliams said to Ernie.

Muffin felt the smooth swerve to the curb, heard the door open and Mr. Willie Williams get out. Leola tried to pull Muffin's head over to her own shoulder but Muffin pulled back and kept her head on Mr. Dale's pressed-flowers shoulder.

Leola started crying. "Why you want to do that, Marvina? Why you want to lay on him and not put your head on your own mother?"

Muffin heard her mother crying again but the crying was not getting inside her; if anything she'd get closer to Mr. Dale.

"She knows I'm the best."

"You! You the best!"

"Right! Me and God—no disrespect to God, God understands."

"But you ain't her mother. Me, I'm her mother. Marvina don't do nothing wrong to nobody; I'm the one bad luck to her. Marvina can't see and that's me too. I got a aunt can't see. That's where it come from, from me. I'm the one don't want no eyes."

"Christ, Leola! Sit up front. Go ahead. Get in front! Muffin doesn't need to sit here listening to you moan. Nobody's moaning tonight—Muffin's alive! If anything we'll have a Blackshout—joyshout, be happy. Won't be no moaning tonight!"

Muffin heard Mr. Willie Williams get back in the car. "I bought some ice cream," he said. "For Muff and the boy."

"Good man!"

"Mr. Dale?" Muffin suddenly asked.

"What, sweet Black angel?"

"Can you ride a horse backward?"

Mr. Dale looked down at Muffin and she didn't move her face but dug her head deeper into his shoulder. "Ride the damn thing any way you want," he said quietly, finally. "If that's what you want."

"Don't curse my child."

Mr. Dale ignored Leola and spoke again to Muffin, his voice feeling soft to her. "I figure if the horse is yours, you ride the way you want to ride."

"You don't know nothing about a horse, Dale! You can't talk to my baby about no horses. You ain't never been on no horse, ain't never been *near* no horse!"

"You are ridiculous! Do you know how ridiculous you sound, Leola? I mean, you really are ridiculous. That's why I love you with your ridiculous self!"

"I ain't got no love for you—what I need with your love!"

"Home," Mr. Willie Williams said when Muffin felt the car stop. She didn't feel a crowd, didn't feel the closeness of people. There was an emptiness outside the car.

"Willie, tell Dale the kind of love I got! He can't get the love I got! Tell him how people used to look at me and Marvin in Nashville when we walk side by side. When I was with him, I was tall as Lookout! Tell him, Willie, tell him the kind of love I got—me and Marvin!"

"We can talk about that upstairs, Leola. We can't talk downstairs in the street."

"Marvin didn't do no jiving," Mr. Dale was saying. "He had a lot of smarts, that's what I liked. He didn't jive."

"You jive, Dale—plain old country jive. You think you city jive but you country jive to me. Marvina think you God! But you ain't. You ain't God to me!"

"Sit still," Mr. Dale whispered to Muffin and got out of the car. She heard him walk around to where her mother was. "I think you God, Leola," he said. "Come on."

"I ain't coming nowhere with you, I'm going in my house with my child. Plus, I ain't God. I'm me."

"You talk like God."

"That ain't no sign of nothing!"

Muffin heard Mr. Dale whisper something to Ernie and then turn around and wrap his arms tight about Leola. Muffin could hear her mother struggling and cursing, could hear Mr. Dale kiss her and laugh and kiss her again.

"Move, Dale, damn it!"

Muffin heard Mr. Dale let her mother go and heard her lean in the car. "Come on, Marvina! Here—let Momma help you, and you and that child let's go upstairs and eat the ice cream Willie bought."

"I'm taking her for a ride," Ernie said. "Maybe Coney Island."

"Oh, well, oh," Leola said and helped Muffin out the back seat and into the front seat and hugged her and mussed her hair and Muffin didn't care.

Mr. Dale handed her his wooden pic and then walked around to Ernie's side and Muffin heard him flip open his wallet. "Fill the tank," he said.

Muffin heard Ernie's leather jacket twist when he turned toward Mr. Dale. "It's full," he said.

"Great," Mr. Dale said. "That's what I like—people who don't need my money!" But Muffin knew he really wanted Ernie to take it.

Mr. Dale slapped the top of the car. "Get Muffin out of here," he said.

Ernie put the car in first gear and pulled away from the curb and Muffin felt the flow of the street beneath her, felt the sound of Ernie changing gears, felt the way his leather jacket crackled against the worn plastic covered seatback, felt the way he was leaning and driving cramped so he could keep an arm around her.

Coney Island was icy, whipping, stinging wind.

"You sure you want to walk—"

"Yes."

The wind slapped her and her ankles were frozen and her pea jacket wasn't warm any more and her ears were

147

numb and her small earrings were missing and she walked through wind making sounds like Mr. Thomas and safe sounds like Ernie's arms tighter around her and Muffin cried for the first time that day and the wind blew the tears against her ears and under her collar and down Ernie's stiff cold leather lapel.

"Okay?"

"I'm okay."

And for a while the tears stopped and she felt like talking but when she tried, the tears started again. "You know, Ernie," Muffin cried, her words breaking off in places, struggling. "I know I'm not pretty and I'm plain and I'm too skinny and I'm too tall and I can't see. But I felt so pretty and the dress turned out and I didn't make any mistakes and I was going upstairs to show Mr. Dale how I looked and when the man said, 'Little yellow riding hood,' at first I smiled— I smiled a little and I was getting ready to tell him I made the dress and—I knew he was Black. Remember before when it happened to Queenie and the man was white—but the man wasn't white this time."

The wind was burning her face. Her nose was running and her head ached.

"He was Black. And poor Mr. Thomas, he's so old and he kept hitting the man with a strap and the man hit him so bad and had a knife and cut him too and Mr. Thomas kept falling and getting up and hitting him and then the man left and he didn't run and Mr. Thomas can't talk and nobody even knew it and then Mr. Dale came and Momma woke up and screamed and then Miss Geneva came and everybody and the police came."

"And I came," Ernie said, "and Mr. Williams came. And both of us got lost getting to a hospital the two of us can get to blindfolded!"

"People will talk about me the way they talked about Queenie."

When they were back in the car again and Ernie was taking her home, Muffin was still talking—couldn't stop. "Ernie," she said, "when you came by and rang the bell, I knew it was you but I just wanted to wear my dress and go up and show Mr. Dale. And maybe if I had let you visit me this wouldn't have happened."

Then Muffin began to cry again and she sat still and not against Ernie and she let the tears run down her face and she didn't try to wipe them away and she knew this would be the last time she cried about it.

"What about Kwanza?" Ernie asked. "I have a little money—"

"Tomorrow's Christmas Eve, Ernie."

"I know. But the stores are open and maybe we can find a dress you like. I'll pick you up in the morning and we'll shop and I won't talk about horses."

"And after Christmas Day it won't be Kwanza for me. I don't believe in Kwanza anymore. It's not true all that stuff Daddy said about Black people—because Black people hurt each other and they don't love each other and if you have a pretty yellow velvet dress you sewed all day, somebody comes in the hall and tears it up and bothers you and beats up a real old man and Daddy was wrong when he said all that other stuff. I shouldn't have believed him!" She was crying again.

"He wasn't wrong."

149

"He was, Ernie! He was!"

"He wasn't wrong."

"Black people even killed him!"

"He wasn't wrong, Muffin."

I wish I was double dead.

"People are people," Ernie said. "They do what they do."

EIGHTEEN

"That don't make no sense you sitting around, Marvina. Sitting around doing nothing—just looking!"

"I'm not doing *nothing*, Momma. It's only Christmas Eve but I've cooked the whole dinner for tomorrow already. I cooked the turkey, and I stuffed it with the corn bread dressing you like. I made the rolls. I baked the macaroni and cheese, and cooked stringbeans, and I dumped pineapples on the ham and baked that too. Everything is done. Tomorrow I'll just heat up and Mr. Willie Williams and Miss Geneva will have a good dinner and you and me too." Muffin opened her watch. "It's seven thirty," she announced, "and I did everything I planned. It worked out perfect. And now I'm going to bed!"

"Nobody told you to do all that, you just jumped and did it. You didn't have to cook no Christmas dinner Christmas Eve! I was going to do it but you just upped and did it! Why you do that, Marvina?"

"You went out this morning crying, Momma, and when you came back you were high and you went to sleep and you slept and woke up and cried and kept on crying. I don't know why you're crying. I'm not."

"I got to cry, Marvina. What else I can do! I got to cry!"

"I'm not." *Ever!*

Muffin heard her mother open the closet and take her coat out and she didn't want to fuss but she had to ask, "Where are you going, Momma?"

Leola didn't answer.

Muffin, feeling suddenly and deeply sad, asked again. "Momma, where are you going?"

"Out."

"Stay in, Momma. You were sick again last night after Ernie and I came back. You were drinking the whole time we were in Coney Island and Mr. Dale made me go to bed and I wanted to sleep and I couldn't sleep with you sick like that. Don't go drink, Momma."

"I got to go cause I can't stand to see you just sit and look and don't say nothing!" Muffin heard her curse then. "And I don't need to 'go' drink! I got a drink here if I want a drink!" She was putting on her coat. "One thing I hope, I hope I don't see that child. That boy been trying to come see you all day and you telling me to tell him you sleep don't mean nothing. He know you ain't sleep. I can see it in his eyes, he know you ain't sleep!"

Muffin had wanted to talk to Ernie, had wanted to see him and didn't want to see him. What was there to talk about?

"Why don't you go up, see Dale? Dale ain't done nothing to you."

"I don't feel like it. Anyway, he said he was coming down here tonight to see me. If he doesn't, it'll be okay. I don't want to see anybody!"

Leola grabbed hold of her daughter and held tight and Muffin stood there and let her and felt nothing so deeply that there was no meaning to her mother's arm wrapped about her. The thin arms held her tighter but they had nothing to do with Muffin's real self, her blood self, her brain self. She stood stiffly, feeling the nubby uneven tweed of her mother's good coat against her bare arms.

"I'm scared, Marvina."

"Then don't go out, Momma. Stay here."

"Why you giving up, baby? Fight back! Don't be like me—get to be a sad old woman."

"You're just thirty-six, Momma."

"I give up. You can't give up. You young!"

Didn't her mother understand there was no way to stop things, no way to change things that happened?

"Don't you give up, Marvina! It'll kill me if you give up. The man didn't do everything he could done to you —the doctor say he didn't do nothing! You don't have no reason acting like this!"

I just don't care much, Momma, Muffin thought. I just don't care. She could easily have said it out loud but she didn't want her mother to feel worse, drink harder. But what happens, happens, Muffin said inside herself.

"It's me the bad luck to you. So the bad luck going out the door, the bad luck going."

"Do what you want, Momma," Muffin said. "You never listen to me." Muffin pulled away from her

153

mother and walked down the hall and heard her mother open the door and go out in the hall and walk down the steps. Thin, small footsteps.

Suddenly, Muffin wanted to leave too. To go out, to escape.

She put on her pea jacket and unhooked her cane from the wooden pineapple, took her glasses from the plastic tusks of the dresser elephant and walked out of her room and walked out of her apartment and shut the door and did not double-bolt it.

In the hallway, Muffin looked up toward Mr. Thomas's and thought of all the presents she'd wrapped that day and of his, and hoped for a moment she'd hear him open his door. But he didn't. She had wanted to go and say something to him but she had not. What do you say to an old man who couldn't talk, who only peeked at people, who came to defend you with a musty, peeling belt against big rhinoceros skin fists and a short, click-in, click-out knife?

Better to stay away.

Muffin, outside now, was not surprised to find herself walking toward The New Church of Mr. Willie Williams. Her fingers opened the watch cover and read eight twelve. "It's Christmas Eve," Muffin said quietly to herself. "And I want to go to church."

When Muffin opened the new glass door of the storefront church, the sound of tambourines and two pianos and many Black voices—rising and falling—doing magical things, poured out to meet her and brought her in.

Muffin sat down in the back.

Williams was saying, his voice getting louder. "Look to yourself and you'll find God! Touch yourself and you touch God! Feel, feel, feel your mouth. God's mouth! Feel your eyes. God's eyes! Raise, lift your hands—lift your hands to help somebody! God's hands! Open your ears to people, to what people need. God's ears! Let somebody lean on your shoulders. God's shoulders! Your shoulders are God's shoulders! Your shoulders are God's shoulders like your body is God's body and your spirit is God's spirit. And God is you! And you are God!

"And this is Christmas and you must be your Black-GodSelf and be born again. Be reborn! Be Born Again and give birth to your Godself again!

"Go out and find somebody and that somebody, tell that somebody—say: You are God! Tell that somebody he's God! Say you are God and God can't be wrong, can't be ugly! And then you and somebody you found, go out and find somebody else and the two of you tell him, tell him, tell him he is God! You are God! You're God! You are, you are, you are God! And God is perfect, He is Black and He is Perfect to me, a Perfect Black to me. God is BlackPerfect, BlackBlack, PerfectPerfect, Black and Perfect and Perfect and Black to me. And I am Black and you are Black and we must be God and we are God and we must love, give Perfect Love and if we give Perfect Love to each other, we can't give wrong to each other. Can't do no wrong, can't be anything but BlackPerfect, PerfectBlack!"

Muffin listened to Mr. Willie Williams talk about the Black Madonna and the Black Christ and she heard the music and she felt a rush of something inside, a bursting

155

of something and it was good to her and she reached
in and held it there as long as she could and she was not
surprised to find herself singing too. Not surprised she
knew the words of songs she never remembered hearing
before:

> *I had a little book, an' I read it through,*
> *I got my Jesus as well as you;*
>
> *I know I would like to read, like to read,*
> *Like to read a sweet story of old;*
>
> *I got a letter this mornin'*
> *—Aye, Lawd*
>
> *My Lord's writing all the time.*

Songs tumbled out of her:

> *O stay in the field, childeren-ah,*
> *Stay in the field, childeren-ah,*
> *Stay in the field*
> *Until the war is ended.*
>
> *I've got my breastplate, sword, and shield,*
> *And I'll go marching thro' the field,*
> *Till the war is ended.*
>
> *Oh, my feet are shod with the gospel grace,*
> *And upon my breast a shield;*
> *And with my sword I intend to fight*
> *Until I win the field.*

Kwanza wove its way into Muffin's self and for the
first time in forever, she wanted to go again.

What she wore wasn't important.

When Muffin and Mr. Willie Williams went back to her house, her mother was sitting by the door in a kitchen chair. Mr. Willie Williams walked in first and Leola didn't see Muffin squeeze past him and go in her room and shut her door. "Willie!" she heard her mother say. "Willie, go find my child! Willie—she gone. I'm waiting for her and Marvin. Marvina gone! Willie, find my child!"

"Leola, Muff's here! The girl's back there in her room!"

"Marvina gone. Marvina running like I ran. Marvina gone."

Muffin flipped her pillow over hard and sank deep into it, but late that night when midnight came and it was Christmas, she was awake with tears rushing down her face. She was neither crying for herself or because of the hallway. She wasn't thinking about her father either. The tears had just come and she had not tried to stop them.

Muffin stayed in bed all of Christmas Day except to heat up the food she had prepared the day before and to eat dinner with her mother and Mr. Willie Williams and Miss Geneva. Her mother had invited Mr. Thomas but he hadn't come down. Mr. Willie Williams had left to visit some sick people and Miss Geneva was trying to get her mother to play the new record player but she wouldn't. "I play it when I'm by myself," she kept saying. "That's the way I like it. Go home, Geneva! You got a home and I got a home. Go home!"

Muffin woke up once and thought she heard Ernie's voice, thought she heard Mr. Dale. She did.

She closed her eyes again tight and pretended to be asleep.

"Marvina! Marvina!" her mother was yelling, running down the hall. She opened the door and came in and flopped heavily by Muffin. "Marvina, wake up! Come see the dress Dale made so you and that child can go to the party you want! That Kwanza stuff!" Leola leaned over and tried to hug Muffin and she slipped a little and fell forward and the room smelled stuffed up with the sours of whisky to Muffin and she kept pretending sleep, wishing to go back to sleep again.

"Marvina!"

Muffin was trying to get up and get away from her mother's bone-thin, smothering arms when she heard Mr. Dale call her. Heard him walking down the hall toward her.

"Hurry, Marvina! The boy already dressed. Marvina!"

"Hi, Ernie," Muffin managed, when she smelled the wet summer forest in her room. But she pulled the covers up higher about her old flannel pajamas before she said hi to Mr. Dale. She was about to whisper something else to him so he could make everybody get out of her room.

But she couldn't.

Mr. Dale had handed her something, laid it heavily upon her bed and her fingers, her hands had made a mistake. Surely, they had made an error. Feel again. Touch. She knew the smell.

158   The pale pink suede.

A long dress, a wrap-around tied with very thin leather strips of more pale pink suede. And a long matching cape. The box on top of it all held a pair of satin shoes, wedge-heeled and ankle-strapped. Mr. Dale said they were black. The stockings too. As well as a long, completely lace, slip. Then Mr. Dale gave her the longest narrowest box she had ever felt in her life and she unwrapped it and opened it and took out the fine slim cane and it didn't have scratched-in names and it wasn't wood. The handle, delicately shaped into a woman's fist, screwed off. Inside, written in Braille, was a note. It read:

Strut.

"Sterling silver and special made just for you," Mr. Dale said and kissed her on the lips and she was crying now and couldn't stop and wouldn't let go of him, and her mother's thin hair was pressed against her face too.

"Happy Kwanza, Black diamond girl," Mr. Dale said.

NINETEEN

SHE WAS IN THE SAME TUB, using the same milk bath powder of dried, precious flowers, and she could hear some of the same voices she had heard in her house two nights ago.

Except that it was not panne velvet on the door but pink suede.

Muffin got out of the tub and cleaned it and dried herself and used the lotion Mr. Dale had brought down for her, but she didn't rub it in the way he had told her. Whether or not it brought a "magic soft" to her skin didn't matter to her. What mattered was that her mother was still drinking. Muffin tried to close down her mind while she put on the long black lace slip. She pulled on the sheer, fine black panty hose and stuck her feet into the clumsy, funny-feeling satin shoes and buckled the extremely thin straps across her ankles. Then she took the pink suede dress off its hanger and slipped into its un-lined heaviness and tied it around her with the long leather strips.

It was exactly like the lemon yellow panne velvet. She was the one that was different.

Muffin combed her hair and patted it and sat down on the edge of the bathtub and thought about her mother. This night might get really bad for her. Would her mother be drinking too much and would she leave the house after everybody had gone?

After a while, Muffin opened the bathroom door and walked down the hallway, through her mother's room, to the living room.

"Black Muffin-girl!" She heard Mr. Dale exclaim and clap his hands once and snap his fingers. "Strut, baby! Don't you walk. Strut—strut your Kwanza on in!"

Muffin heard Ernie laughing.

And she heard her mother pour a drink and then put the bottle back on the glass part of the coffee table. "I got to take a drink on this—Marvina beautiful!"

"Always beautiful," Mr. Dale said, guiding her and sitting her down in the wing-backed chair. "Later for 'I Got It Bad and That Ain't Good.' Put on 'Satin Doll'—the Duke knew what he was talking when he wrote that thing."

"You think you a satin doll," her mother said while she was changing the record. Muffin heard her mother's lips making a sound and knew she was poking out her tongue at Mr. Dale.

"Can, if I want to be," he said and walked over and kissed her and came back and began to part Muffin's hair.

"What I tell you about kissing me! What I want with your kisses!"

"Best thing ever happened to you, Leola! And hush! I have to concentrate on Muffin's hair."

161

Leola came over and leaned on Muffin and wrapped her arms partly about her hair.

"I can't do her hair and braid in these black glass beads with you slopping all over her! Damn, Leola!" he cried, and undid her hands and arms about Muffin.

"Braid all you want. That's MY child! She the one making that dress look good, that dress ain't doing it! How about that? Put that in your pipe and smoke it!"

"Leola!" Mr. Dale almost screamed. "Move! Get away—get away! You going crazy as hell!"

"How you know, you must be crazy too," Muffin heard her mother say, felt her hug Mr. Dale hard. "Takes one to know one!"

Muffin listened to her mother and Mr. Dale fussing with each other and Mr. Willie Williams was back and listening to them too. Ernie was laughing a little.

Mr. Dale moved back and forth cornrowing Muffin's hair and she wanted to tell him that she really didn't want to go, that she could feel Kwanza even if she stayed at home, that she was worried about her mother—alone tonight with all the medicine she had put away herself and wouldn't tell where it was, and alone with her whisky and alone with her memories of last Christmas night.

But she couldn't say all this to him. He was so happy.

"Listen to Africa!" Mr. Dale cried when he finally finished. "Listen to Africa come in here!" He grabbed Leola and danced her about for a minute. "Look at Muffin! Look at Africa sitting over there!"

Muffin put her hands up and felt the rows and rows of braids and small glass beads going upward toward

162

the center of her head and ending in a twisted spike.

"My God," Mr. Dale cried. "You didn't polish your fingernails!" Ten minutes later, he was putting his clear polish on her freshly shaped fingernails. He wiped her glasses with lens cleaner and then handed her the new, skinny, silver cane. "I don't know what to say to you, baby," he said. "You look so good, I don't know what to say." He put his arms around her and drew her close. "Have yourself a natural ball," he said. "Be sure all the little boys—that one over there included—know you the best! Don't stop till they know it!"

"What kind of thing is that you done with Marvina's hair?" her mother said when he let her go.

"You can't understand it, Leola!"

Moments later, Muffin was going down the steps, holding up the long dress. Mr. Willie Williams, Mr. Dale, and Miss Geneva were all in the hall. "Good-by, everybody," Leola was saying, much to Muffin's horror. "Marvina got her party and I got my quiet cause tonight's my night. This me and Marvin's night and I don't want to see nobody. Everybody go home! Don't come back in my house!"

"You have a precious piece of Black sitting there beside you," Mr. Dale said to Ernie when they were in the car."

"I got it," Ernie said.

"Yeah, I know you know you got it."

"You don't look so happy," Ernie said when they had dropped off Mr. Willie Williams and were on their way to pick up three of Ernie's small sisters.

"I don't want to go. I'm only going because Mr. Dale   163 took the material he was saving so long for his own self and made me this dress. It wouldn't be right not to go."

"He loves you."

"I love him too, Ernie. Except for my mother and father, I think I love him the best and next is Mr. Willie Williams. And now I think I love Mr. Thomas. I wanted to go up and say Merry Christmas to him but I didn't know what to say. I even bought a present for him the other day, but I just don't want to go up there. Momma invited him to eat dinner with us and I wanted him to come but he didn't. I think it's because Momma was real high when she asked him."

"Why didn't you ask him yourself?"

"I didn't want to see anybody, Ernie! All I wanted was to get dinner over with and out the way. At dinner, all Momma did was fuss at Mr. Willie Williams. And he didn't say anything. She hardly let him say grace, saying, 'Don't sit here and eat my food and thank Jesus. Jesus didn't cook that food, Marvina cooked that food!' "

"That's kind of funny," Ernie said.

"It's not funny, Ernie," Muffin said, "Momma kept playing Duke Ellington's 'Mood Indigo,' saying Daddy wanted to hear it and then she kept playing over and over, 'I Got It Bad and That Ain't Good.' So as soon as I washed the dishes I went back to bed and I told Mr. Willie Williams to tell you if you came I was sleep or up Mr. Dale's. And then Mr. Dale was there and you were with him."

"He came to the store and asked if I wanted an outfit free—to match the one he was making you. I told 164   him no and what you had said about not going to

Kwanza and he said, 'She's going.' Told me to ring his bell before I picked you up and I did."

"I really don't want to go, Ernie. Can we just ride?"

"No."

"I'm serious!"

"I'm serious too."

"People better not start asking me questions about that man."

"They won't."

"They will, Ernie!"

"They have to get through me first," he said. "And I don't think they can."

Ernie's three small sisters piled in the car, and Muffin felt fake fur against her throat, her face. Icy cheeks. Hands in her hair. "You look real *pretty*," Amina said. "I can cornrow too, I'm the only one in the second grade can do it. You look *real* pretty."

"Watch this," Ernie said and leaned over and kissed Muffin and Muffin didn't think the three girls would ever stop squealing.

"I'm telling Momma," Asa declared.

"That's cause you a tattletale."

"I'm not talking to you, Ede!"

"You know what, Ernie?" Muffin asked when they finally pulled into the parking lot of the Black Museum.

"What?"

"I keep thinking about that horse and I've decided the best way to ride *is* backward. So I'm not going to worry when you say it from now on. When you ride backward, you only see the good stuff that already happened and you can keep your eye on that."

165

"Don't you need to see where you're going?"

"All I want to see is where I been."

But when Muffin walked through the door and heard the drums and heard Deeta yell, "Muffin! Your dress— your dress! I can't *believe* you in that dress. And the cape!" and turned her face up toward the ceiling and imagined the way the black mobiles looked—laden with the glue and sparkles she had sprinkled, she forgot about horses. She even forgot her disappointment when Deeta told her she had missed hearing Etta Moten Barnett and the Black writer John Oliver Killens. "He was *real* good," Deeta said.

As soon as Ernie checked Muffin's cape he put his arms around her and held her and danced her all around the room. And whirling about in the darkness with him, doing the Soul Train, she forgot about the scent of dried, pressed, extraordinary flowers and thought the very best thing of all was a forest wet with summer rain.

Ears of corn were being given to everybody and Ernie gave her one. "Remember," he said, "tonight an ear of corn is called *muhindi*. More than one—you say *mihindi*."

"I know, Ernie. I was in the class too."

At ten minutes to twelve, Muffin heard the voice of Sekou—who used to be Roger Anderson—the fourteen-year-old manboy sage who practically ran the Black Museum.

The drums went into a frenzy, heralding the coming of Kwanza. Then abruptly they halted, and Muffin heard Sekou speak again.

"He's putting down the straw mat," Ernie said.

Sekou's voice thundered, "*Mkeka.* Symbolizing the foundation of the Black nation."

The drums answered him in a long roll.

"*Kinara.*"

"The candleholder?" Muffin asked.

"Right."

"See the stalk," Sekou said. "The original stalk—symbolizing the one origin from which we all came."

Drums. Another roll, louder than the first.

"The stalk of the candle, Ernie, is the handle. The part all seven of the candleholders are attached to."

"*Mishumaa,*" Sekou announced, and Muffin knew he had picked up the seven black candles—decorated at the base with flowing satin streamers of red, black, and green—that she had touched just last week. "These candles," she heard Sekou's voice boom, "represent the Seven Principles of Kwanza."

"The *Nguzo Saba,* Ernie."

"*NGUZO SABA!*"

It was hard to hear Sekou's voice calling out each principle as he placed the candles in the Kinara. The drums and the people answered him and it was deafening to Muffin's ears and she reached for and held Ernie's hand to ease the sound.

"*UMOJA.* Unity!"

Drum rolls, people repeating. "*UMOJA!* Unity!"

"*KUJICHAGULIA.* Self-determination."

Drum rolls. "*KUJICHAGULIA!* Self-determination!"

"*UJIMA.* Collective work and responsibility!"

Drum rolls. "*UJIMA!* Collective work and responsibility!"

167

"*UJAMAA*. Cooperative economics."

Drum rolls. Ede crying, frightened. "*UJAMAA!* Cooperative economics!

"*NIA*. Purpose!"

Drums. "*NIA!* Purpose!"

"*KUUMBA*. Creativity."

Drums. "*KUUMBA!* Creativity!"

"*IMANI*. Faith."

Tremendous drum rolls. "*IMANI!* Faith!"

"Three seconds to twelve," Ernie managed to yell in Muffin's ear amid the powerful, long, tumultuous drum rolls. She didn't need Ernie to tell her when it was finally twelve o'clock and she didn't need to flip open her watch dome. The drums told her in a burst and kept up the pace, and the driving and rhythmic force pulled Muffin along, pulled her into people and pulled her into herself and she heard herself shouting Happy Kwanza to faces she couldn't see. Hugging people. Being hugged. Heard Ernie's sisters shouting Happy Kwanza and she wanted to pick one up and they weren't there.

Ernie was. "Happy Kwanza," he said.

"Happy Kwanza, Ernie," she yelled.

"There're only seven drummers up there," Ernie shouted to her. "You ought to see!"

I can see them Ernie, she wanted to say. I swear I can see them! I even saw Sekou light that first candle.

Then suddenly the drums halted, and moments later the people heard the great quiet. And when there was absolute silence, Muffin heard Sekou's deep voice, measured, paced, go out to all of them. "Happy Kwanza," he said. "This is not new. This celebration is not new. This is an old celebration—it is a tradition. It is a tradition among Black African people. We are celebrating and our brothers and sisters in the Motherland—in Africa—are celebrating. And all this is not new. We did this together hundreds of years, centuries, *before* the Christ was born. Kwanza is our ancestors meeting to feast the harvesting of the first crops, *centuries* before the Christ was born.

"It is not new.

"This is not a new thing. Kwanza is not new. You are not a new people, you are an old people. You didn't begin in 1619. You had a history, you *have* a history. You had *programmed* festivals hundreds of years *before* the Christ was born! Let us now continue. Let us now continue our old celebrations. The slave ships will not interrupt this one.

"The first fruits we emphasize here today—are the young people. They are the beginning of nations. Think on this for these seven days. Think of the young when we have our final *karamu*—on the seventh day. Think of the young when we drink from the *Kikombe*, the Unity Cup—when we drink the wine. Think of the young as the gifts of Black mothers and Black fathers together in love. Giving. *Zawadi*—"

"*Zawadi* is gift," Muffin whispered.

"*Mihindi*," Sekou said deeply. "*Mihindi*. The ears of corn. Bring your ears of corn forward and lay them on the *Mkeka* until it overflows. We want it to overflow. We will make it overflow. One ear of corn to represent each child in the family. And if there are no

169

children in your family—place one ear of corn upon the mat to signify the children who will come.

And it was while Muffin was placing her ear of corn on top of the huge pile, people pressing close, her hand in Ernie's, that she felt something delicate emerge within her and get stronger and spread. And she knew what it was. This grand thing pulling her forward, making her want to reach out and touch faces, hug people, hold people. They weren't strangers, they were hers. She belonged to them, had always belonged to them, and they belonged to her.

What she felt was strength.

It was a knowing time for her, a time of understanding.

To be Black was to be strong, to have courage, to survive. And it wasn't an alone thing. It was family. It was her father automatically trusting two Black men. It was a crumbling old man coming out of his safe place into a danger place. It was a man who knew everything and had everything, giving it to her, letting her butt into his life whenever she wanted. It was a preacher saying God was Black and you are God. It was a lady finding her life in other families, helping them. It was a boy being a man all the time. It was her mother.

It was as precious as that.

And when the drums began again, they began for her.

"Ernie," Muffin said. "I feel good." But she knew he hadn't heard her, it was too noisy to hear her but she said it anyway and took her place in the large circle that was forming.

Muffin held on to Ernie's hand and held Amina's on

the other side but Ede wanted Muffin to hold hers too. So Muffin let go of Ernie's hand for the first time that night and reached for Ede's. She felt Ernie reach down and pick up Asa and put her on his shoulders.

The fingers of the little girls felt so small in hers. It was easy to hold somebody's hand and sometimes you just had to do it—as people had done for her.

The circle was completed and it was silent. Muffin waited.

"We are silent now," Sekou said, "for the people who have gone, left the field. Some are dead," he said. "But others live, walk in your midst, exist on the outside. We know they will come back. We will welcome them back.

There was only one drum now and it was wailing and Muffin wanted to go home.

But she danced with Ernie one more time. "I feel good," she told him when the music stopped and he could hear.

"You look good," he said.

"Wow, Ernie!" she said, feeling kind of silly. Why hadn't she just said thank you? She did then. But it was time to go. "Ernie," she asked, "where's Deeta?"

"I know," Ede yelled. "I'll go get Deeta for you!"

"No," Muffin said. "Take me where she is."

"What's the matter?" Ernie asked.

"I have to go to the ladies' room!"

"You know where it is and you can get to it without Deeta's help. What's wrong?"

"Oh, brother!"

"Okay," Ernie said. "Okay."

171

"Come on!" Ede yelled, and grabbed Muffin's hand. "Deeta might move!"

Muffin followed the little girl through the pulsing, tangled crowd and shook her head when she could tell that Ede was pushing people aside. "Move!" Ede shouted time and time again. "We can't see!"

When Muffin was finally at Deeta's side, she reached down and kissed Ede's small cheek. "Tell Ernie I'm turning my horse around," she said. "Tell him I'm riding forward. Front."

"You got a horse?"

"No," Deeta said. "Muffin ain't got no horse. What Muffin got is the toughest dress here!"

"It's a special horse. Ernie'll know."

"Okay," Ede said. "Go tell him now?"

"No, Ede. Wait till you see me with my cape on, going out the door."

"She can stay with me," Deeta said. "I'll take her back when you go."

"Tell me what you'll say to Ernie, Ede?"

"You said you have to ride your horse front."

"That's it," Muffin said. "That's good."

And with Deeta and Ede watching Ernie closely, Muffin was able to get her cape and cane and leave. They all stood inside the drafty vestibule of the museum until Deeta, wearing Muffin's cape and running back and forth, finally hailed a cab.

"You can wear the cape home, Deeta, if you want to."

"I know you must be crazy, Muffin! My mother's in there—she'd kill me!"

The first thing Muffin did when she got back to her house was to go up Mr. Thomas's apartment. She knocked on the door late as it was and when he opened it—in a musty threadbare woolen bathrobe—and unhooked the chain, she put her arms around him and hugged him and felt the massive bandage on his face. "Happy Kwanza," she said and hugged him so hard that time that she couldn't breathe for a moment and he hugged her back and made a few sounds that weren't strange to her, sounds she thought she understood.

Muffin pulled away and said thank you—"For everything, Mr. Thomas." And told him about the present that she'd bring up tomorrow and touched his face and hugged him again. She told him she was sorry it was so late but that she had gone to the Kwanza celebration and she was going to tell him all about it and what it meant, if he felt like being bothered with her. She told him that on the seventh and final day of Kwanza, she was going to come and get him and take him to the Karamu, the big feast. And she told him to come and visit her and her mother any time he wanted and she, Muffin, would come up and visit him. Then she told him not to pay any attention to what her mother said because she just talked like that. Then Muffin kissed him and felt his tears and she kissed him again and reached over and touched Mr. Dale's door and went downstairs.

It was time to go to her mother.

She wouldn't talk to her about horses. She, Muffin, would give what she knew, could understand finally.

Strength, and survival. And going on.

173

TWENTY

"Marvina, leave me be!"

"Go ahead and cry, Momma," Muffin said. "I'll just sit here on the side of your bed and keep on brushing your hair."

"I ain't crying, I'm trying to see if I see Marvin. If I lay here and lay here, maybe he come."

"He can't, Momma."

"He coming! He coming. All I got to do is watch."

"We don't need Daddy any more."

"Shut up, Marvina! He coming—he here! I know he here!"

"Daddy's not here, Momma, and he's never going to come back again. He can't give us anything else."

Leola pulled away from Muffin's hands and the comb fell to the floor, and when Muffin reached down to pick it up she felt the almost empty bottle. "Don't touch it," her mother said, when Muffin picked it up. "You got what *you* got and I got what I got. Put my bottle down by my bed. And you get off my bed—get off me! Go back to that Kwanza you been dying for. Ain't nobody told you come home messing with me!"

"You're my Kwanza, Momma."

"I ain't nobody. I ain't nothing!"

"Mr. Dale said you're beautiful."

"Dale saying that cause you can't see!"

"I believe him, Momma."

"You believe. You keep on believing everything everybody tell you—see if they don't make you a fool."

"We're going back to the clinic."

"Shut up, Marvina—"

"And if it doesn't help, we'll find another."

"Marvina! You know what?"

"What, Momma?"

"You don't make no damn sense! Put my bottle down—where you put my bottle? Hand it here!"

"You don't need this tonight. You got me."

"Who you think you talking to, Marvina?"

"And we're strong."

"That ain't no sign of nothing!"

"Yes it is."

"What it a sign of! Damn it!"

"That I love you, Momma."

Two hours later, her mother asleep, with her head cradled in Muffin's lap, Muffin continued to brush the wispy hair and hoped her strength was strong enough.

ABOUT THE AUTHOR

SHARON BELL MATHIS was born in Atlantic City, New Jersey, and grew up in Bedford Stuyvesant, Brooklyn. She and her husband and daughters live in Washington, D. C., where Mrs. Mathis is a special education teacher at Stuart Junior High School. She is also Writer-in-Residence at Howard University, serves on the Board of Advisors, Lawyers Committee, D. C. Commission on the Arts, writes a monthly column for Ebony Jr!, and is former head of the children's division of the D. C. Black Writers' Workshop.

Sharon Bell Mathis is the author of Sidewalk Story, which received an award from the Council on Interracial Books for Children; Teacup Full of Roses, an ALA Notable Book; and The Hundred Penny Box.

About the writing of Listen for the Fig Tree, she says, "Say the same thing about all my books—say that I write to salute Black kids."